Death by fire
The abduction of Liah Singh

Death by fire

Adrian Hamilton

Published by Adrian Hamilton, 2024.

This is a work of fiction. Similarities to real people, places, or events are entirely coincidental.

DEATH BY FIRE

First edition. May 22, 2024.

ISBN: 979-8224723867

Written by Adrian Hamilton.

Adrian Hamilton

The names in this book are all fictitious, and so are the historical events, places mentioned, and names of people. If the names mentioned are part of your first or last names, it was not meant to hurt you, or anyone you may know. All names, characters and places are products of the Author's imagination.

Acknowledgement

A special thanks to my children, grandchildren, Great-grand son, siblings, and friends who encourage me to continue writing this book, when I was about to give up, writing my first crime story. Thanks to you all for believing in me.

It was 5:00 am Monday, February 5th 2011. The bright light flashed through the trees at a distance not very far from the farmhouse. What seems at first like the sun shining against a mirror? Was really a vehicle that was set on fire at the side of the road opposite another farmhouse.

It's not quite certain how the vehicle got there, what time it was driven and by whom, after the flames were extinguished, about half an hour after the fire department arrived, the body of a burnt person was found with their hands tied behind their back in the trunk.

It was noticed by the bystanders in the farming community of Carlson Point the fire department came on the scene five minutes after the police arrived. The area of the scene was now taped off, because it was now a crime scene under investigation by the police and fire department.

It was not long before the bystanders that were present as the crowd began arriving at the scene, asking questions among themselves. They wanted to know who was the person the police found burnt in the back of the vehicle was .

This crime took place early that morning, before the sun came up. It was surprising to the farmer that lived close to the incident, and did not see or heard any vehicle that was parked, because their front fence was made of concrete blocks and stood about eight feet high.

It was not until the owner of the farmhouse got a phone call from another neighbour informing him that there was a vehicle on fire in front of his house; after looking outside, he realized it was in fact the case.

The area in this farming location was always a concern, because the amount of trees used for boundaries between the farmers and it's hard to see when any vehicles are driving by, because the trees are used to divide where the property line is, a much suited spot to carry out this kind of crime.

As the day progressed, the police officers doing the investigation began asking questions about the burnt out vehicle, and if anyone saw heard vehicle, vehicles or any person who drove it there. To the police officer's amazement, no one saw or heard any vehicle or vehicles driving by or stopping.

The police officers at this point have their hands full, trying to find the person or persons who have committed this crime. The vehicle was taken away. And the scene of the crime was now a left as a reminder to everyone a burnt patch on the ground, where broken bits of glass and plastic materials laid as waste.

The scene was not vacant and evacuated, a reminder of where a crime took place. The officers were very non-responsive while looking for any clues in trying to solve this crime, which was at their disposal. This showed the police's lack of interest in solving this crime.

Although all the clues were in front of them, they drove away from the scene of the crime and drove back to the station, trying to put together the clues they had which were not enough to solve the crime of the burnt body found in the shell of the burnt vehicle.

The lack of inexperience may not be enough to solve the crime, which could have great implications towards the officers who are in charged with this case. They were no one showing leadership in judgment. The case looks as though it was a normal occurrence, which every day, but it was not.

This crime was a very calculated one in which it was observed and timed. The way the officers looked at this crime may not be solved anytime in the future because leadership was lacking, and it could take time. The newspaper reported the lack of leadership on the case, and the police department was forced to name a new detective who will be in charge and will bring in two new team members.

It's the start of a new day at the station, and the name of the new detectives handling the case was announced during a meeting, and their names were shared with the newspaper, letting the communities in the surrounding areas know the detectives who were now in charged of the investigation.

The lead detective, taking over the case, was chief detective Inspector Dan Browning, his team members were detective Sargent Steve Grant, and detective Sargent Victoria Haynes were now overseeing the investigation of the abduction and burnt body found in the burnt out vehicle.

The chief detective Inspector Dan Browning was in the police force for ten years before being promoted to the homicide unit. He has fifteen years as a chief detective inspector, with several solved cases to his credentials. He is married to a beautiful woman, has three children, two boys that are twins and a beautiful daughter, all in their teens. They live in the adjacent town about fifteen minutes' drive from the station.

The second member of the team is detective Sargent Steve Grant with ten years in the homicide department. He came from the army policing department, and is married to a beautiful woman with two children, all boys who are preteens, lives within walking distance of the station. He is good at what he does, solving crime and is very thorough.

The third member of the team is detective Sargent Victoria Haynes, a beautiful woman, married to a wonderful man and has one child, a daughter of teenage years. She has been in the police force for ten years, five of which were solving cold cases. She brings to the team a lot of experience solving cold cases.

The team's job was to go over every piece of evidence that was gathered at the crime scene and begin interviewing anyone in the farming community at Carlson Point, especially those living on the main road where the vehicle was found, and find out who may have heard or saw anything about any missing person they have not seen the day before or after the crime.

It's now up to the detectives to canvass the farming community, where the victim's body and vehicle were found, and ask questions if anyone heard or saw anything during the night. The detectives had many questions they discussed among themselves. Did she work, and where was she involved with any shady business? That may have cost her to be killed in such a horrible way.

A team of vehicle investigators was thoroughly processing the vehicle, attempting to find any identification stamp that could provide a clue about the vehicle's make and its owner. The code or identification stamp on the vehicle chassis is very important for finding the owner.

Because of the lack of solid clues or identification, the investigation will take some time. The pathologist is in the process trying to make any kind of identification of the victim, and that in itself takes time. Dental records have to be found, and if DNA could be matched, it would help in a good way, but the latter is much in doubt.

With all what is happening, the detectives are hoping someone may have seen this vehicle or any vehicle travelling in the vicinity where the burnt vehicle was found, and they would come with such information. It is unfortunate, nobody in the farming community has any security cameras facing the road which would capture vehicles driving by that could help in solving the crime.

The detectives would have to rely on their knowledge, and instincts doing their due diligence of gathering all the evidence, even if it means returning to the crime scene, and searching the debris left there from the burnt vehicle. The information was not coming forth from the public that the detectives had hoped.

It was a concern in the eyes of the detectives that no one cares to come forward in the farming community where the vehicle was found. They were tension with the police before, where they was an incident of a break-in, and robbery but the police did nothing to investigate that crime, so it's not surprising that no one wants to help the police.

The police and detectives returned to the crime scene and began scraping the burnt spot where the vehicle was, digging and sifting the debris, looking for any clues they had missed initially. They were no break in the case, and the waiting for a response from the vehicle investigators did not happen, but the investigation goes on, and with no information from the public.

The next day, when the detectives came to work, there was a brown envelope addressed to Detective. Inspector Browning. After opening the envelope and reading the contents sent to him by the vehicle investigation team, they identify the vehicle, which was a clue and was very positive.

The news was good about the identification of the vehicle, but was it the owner of the vehicle which was burnt? It was a concern to the detectives, and would know for sure once the pathologist confirm the body as that of the owner and that it was a woman's body that was in the vehicle.

It was a very positive outlook. What we are hoping for was the identification of the victim, so we can match her as the vehicle owner, giving us a village where she lived, and can give my team a reference point where to start our questioning.

I was hoping to receive more information before we all left work for our respectful homes, but it did not happen, but tomorrow is another day, and the outcome would be a very positive one. It's a new day. The birds were chirping. The sky was blue, and the sun shining bright in the sky with no glimpse of any dark clouds signifying rain was eminent.

It was a nice day driving to work. Traffic was moving at a good pace. No accidents at the time I left home, which was around 7:30 am. All was quiet until a fight broke out with two teenagers just before reaching the station and had to stop it before moving on.

I do not understand why best friends could fight each other over a girl. In my days, I would just walk away and let the other person go with her, no matter how much you love her, and how hard it was going to be and feel.

After separating the two individuals, I continued my drive to the station, got to my desk, and waited to hear from the pathologist about the identification of the body, although we knew who the vehicle belongs too, we wanted to make sure the body was truly hers.

The other detectives came in following each other, but Detective Sargent Haynes was holding a brown envelope, walking over handed it to me. Just then, the phone rang. It was the pathologist. Asking me if I received the envelope, and I replied with the answer, Yes! He said it is all there for you. It was a positive match.

The chief detective inspector, Dan Browning, called his team members together, telling them who the person was in the burnt vehicle, and she was indeed the rightful owner of the vehicle. It was the answer he and the team were waiting for, so they can carry on with the investigation hoping to solve the case.

It takes time, and without cooperation from the public, it could take a very long time. The body tat was found in the burnt vehicle was Liah Singh, and she lived not too far from the farming community of Carlson Point, about five miles away in the village of Junctionville at 135 Anita Lane, an area known to the police where a drug lord live by the name of Abdul Sardooh.

The detectives were in position to carry out their investigation of Liah Singh's death by starting where she lived at 135 Anita Lane in the village of Junctionville, and also where the drug lord Abdul Sardooh lived, and believed to be controlling that part of the village.

The police are fully aware of Abdul's capabilities, because of the gang he also controls, and they would do anything for him if he asked them to get something some, and even to get whatever he wants to get his hands on if it means killing.

The detectives had a meeting and discussed asking questions the next day in Junctionville. They all wanted to know more about the area, the gang and Abdul Sardooh, his operations, and exactly what house he lived in.

The detectives wanted to have as much information about the area, and some individuals along with their identities, and who were associated with the gang, and how loyal were they to the drug lord. It was important for them to know before going into the area, and not walking into an unexpected situation.

It was time to get the investigation moving forward because of the deadly implications between the gang and the police, along with all the information they gathered. The day was coming to a close at the station, and we would continue the following day with some serious canvassing in the area where Liah Singh live.

The next day, the three detectives agree on what they need to accomplish. It was to get as much information about the area, and life of Liah Singh, and above all, who her friends were and if she had any enemies.

The morning came and all three detectives were ready to visit the village of Junctionville, and accompanying them were some heavily armed police members (SWAT) for security and protection, because of the area and the drug lord, who control the gang in the area.

All at the station were ready to leave. After driving for about thirty minutes, they arrived at Junctionville, and the detectives proceed to the home where Liah Singh's parents lived, but no one was home. The detectives asked the neighbour and was told they did not know where the family moved.

Launching a drone, the SWAT members accompanying the detectives covertly documented the area through pictures and video, keeping the drug lord and the gang unaware. The detectives continued their canvassing throughout the neighbourhood for five hours, did not get any positive reply, all if not most, did not want to talk for fear of what could happen to them next.

Fear, like a river after a heavy rainfall, permeated the neighbourhood of Junctionville because of the corruption in the area. The entire village was very fearful of the drug lord and his thugs he control, and talking to the police, or detectives could lead to their death.

The detectives or the SWAT members were not aware the houses they visited were being watched by the gang members, which were controlled by the drug lord, and it put fear into each family and their household.

It was about five hours after trying to get anyone to talk about Liah Singh's family the detectives left the area, thinking it was a waste of time, but little did they know lurking in the area and watching their every move, was someone who may have seen, and know something.

The person watching every move the detectives made was a teenage boy about thirteen years old. Everyone in the village thought he was illiterate, could not speak or write, so they called him Moomooboy.

He was treated as such by the gang members, who ordered him around to do their dirty errands for food and a place to sleep at night and a small shed where he could rest his head. The eyes of this individual watched every move that the detectives made, and listened to everyone when their names were mentioned, following them to where their vehicles were parked.

Upon getting back into their vehicles, the detectives were followed by the SWAT members as they drove back to the station, with nothing to show for the time spent canvassing. It felt as though it was a complete and unfruitful waste of working hours.

Thinking the day was a complete waste of working hours, it turned out it may not have. What they were thinking was that no information about Liah Singh's family was happening. They learned about the neighbourhood, and how it was controlled by the drug lord, and the gang members, which put fear into individuals.

An hour after returning to the station, the senior member of the SWAT team called Chief Detective Inspector Dan. Browning, asking for his team to come to his department, and view the pictures and video taken in the area they were walking through, going from house to house.

The detectives were surprised to see so many people watching their every move as they canvassed door to door, trying to get information, but one clip video clip they saw someone following them, which piqued their interest. It was a teenager boy who was looking at them, who they did not see.

It has now piqued their interest, knowing how close they had been watched, and they would like to know who was this individual watching them was, and why? Does he have something that can help with Liah Singh's family and their whereabouts?

The detectives and senior SWAT officer discussed what was the best way to disrupt the gang members' activity, putting them against each other, or arresting them one at a time during the night. The day was not a waste of working hours, but slow progress in the solving of a vicious murder.

It could be away, to get answers, as each gang member is detained for conspiracy, and controlling people by fear and death threats. The detectives and SWAT leader continue their calibration the next day since it was close to going home. They all left with a positive attitude for the next day.

The next day, as the sun raised its brilliant head from the east, and the dazzling reflection shine on the water, looks that it was going to be a great day. At the station, the detectives, along with the SWAT leader, and his team, got together to discuss ways on how they can arrest the gang members one at a time, and have them think the missing member is talking to the police.

The SWAT team have to get a good look at the individuals on the video, get a still photo of them, and pass it on to the detectives, who will look through their database making sure they are known to the police, and their whereabout.

It was given the green light, and everything they talked about, is now a way to get information one individual at a time. This was a way, not only to get information, but to take back the neighbourhood run by the drug lord and his gang.

There was now reason for the operation to go ahead, by the name DRAWIT. A name that is not obvious to anyone, but to law enforcement officers who will carry out the of arresting those gang members, one at a time.

The operation called DRAWIT was going to be begun, when no one expected it. Everyone had to be prepared for a moment's notice. The discussions were over, and the detectives walked back to their office, and opening the door to the station was a teenager boy dressed in dirty clothes, standing at the front desk, asking to speak with detective Dan Browning.

Why do you want to speak with Det. Browning the officer at the front desk asked?

I just want to talk to him the dirty-looking teenager replied Please wait here, the police officer said.

Ok, I will wait here, the dirty teenager replied.

Detective Dan Browning walked out and approached the dirty teenager.

What can I do for you? Detective Browning asked.

It's what I can do for you? He replied.

Go on, I am listening Detective Browning said.

My name is Moomooboy, that's what everyone calls me. They think I cannot speak or hear.

Detective Browning was very interesting in what Moomooboy had to say, and was taken to the interview room, and was monitored by the other two detectives.

Go ahead, what's on your mind? Det. Browning asked.

I saw you and the other two officers going house to house, and I followed you he replied.

Why were you following us? Det. Browning asked.

I have information for you about Liah Singh; he replied.

Are you sure about your facts? Det. Browning asked.

Yes! I am very sure, he replied.

Ok, tell me all that you know, Det. Browning said.

Three nights ago, I overheard a conversation between the drug lord , and three of the gang members to abduct and burn Liah Sing's body in her vehicle.

Go on, what was the reason? Det. Browning asked.

I don't know; she is a schoolteacher, and leaves early to visit an old lady, before going to her teaching job.

Do you know what school she teaches? Det. Browning asked.

Not really. Her parents moved when they were shown a picture of her in the trunk of her vehicle on fire.

How do you know all this information? Det. Browning asked.

My parents are close friends of Liah's parents.

Do you know where they went to? Det. Browning asked.

No, I don't, he replied.

Do you know any of the men responsible for abducting and killing her? Det. Browning asked.

I sure do. I have pictures of them on my phone. Do you want to see? Momoboy asked.

I sure would like that very much? Det. Browning said.

Here they are, he replied.

Can I download these on my computer? Det Browning asked.

Yes, you can, if it would help. He replied.

Thank you very much. I hope you don't get into trouble for coming to the station, Det. Browning said.

No, I won't, they all think. I am dumb. My name is Moomooboy, remember he said.

After Moomooboy left the station, the detectives were now positioned to find the names of the gang members, and the pictures on the phone matching a face to anyone they know or activities they have on file with the police department.

What was looking as the impossible to solve, was now viewed as a possibility, with just a small split, that was not available has now opened into a crack, in the case, and we can now look ahead in solving the crime, and arresting those individuals responsible.

It will take sometime, but the first thing we need to do is identify the names of the individuals pictures that were given to us by Moomooboy. I must say, he was a brave individual to give us the information that could help us solve this case.

I would have never thought, with all the resistance, we were getting into the neighbourhood where Liah lived. Someone was not afraid of what could happen to him, made it his mission to help the detectives with information needed.

The pictures from the phone from Moomooboy matched three of the four, and were surprised the number of warrants were outstanding for them. The fourth individual was not, but we continued our search. After twenty minutes of searching, his picture was found, with another state warrant for murder.

This gave the detectives leverage to expedite a search warrant where they lived, and also the arrest them. The names of the individuals were..

James "Skinny" Wilson,

Peter "Wide mouth" Strong

Vernon "Sneaky" Hinds

Winston "Big belly" Walton

All lived at one house, and the police has now put surveillance watching the house, and their daily movements. The detectives and the SWAT team leader would decide the day and time when operation DRAWIT will take place, which would be a surprise to the four individuals. The details were all worked out and agreed by both teams.

It made sense for us to watch the area of Junctionville village, and bide our time, when the raid on the four individuals would take place. Since it was a good day, with our progress, and the day's work was drawing near, we all tidied up our desks, making sure all the important papers were locked up before leaving for home.

It's a new day, and it's raining cats and dogs, heavily, which is delaying me a little, but it's better not to rush out in the rain. So; I am giving it a little time to see if it will ease, for me to make my way to my vehicle, and get to work safely, rain have not fallen that heavily in a long time.

The rain eased a little, for me, i got to my vehicle and drove to work, but the road had so much pooling water that a vehicle in front of me was going fast, and it hydro-planed into a tree a little way off the sidewalk.

It's lucky, no one was walking in that area which would have caused some serious injury. The vehicle was not seriously damaged, but the driver was shaken up, but OK, and had to wait for the police and a tow truck before he could have the vehicle removed.

I got to the station and had to make a fast dash the entrance, which got me wet a bit, but less than what I was expecting, walked to my office, the other two detectives were not there yet, normally they would arrive before or we arrive at the same time.

To tell you the truth, I don't listen to the weather, but today of all days I turned the radio, and the meteorologist said it was going to rain for most of the day, easing up before the commute drive home. I was just about to sit at my desk when the front desk officer paged me to come up front, there was someone here to see you.

He did not give me a name, so I made my way to the front desk, and sitting down all wet from head to toe, was Moomooboy, who was glad to see me.

What brings you out to the station in all this rain? Det. Browning asked.

I have some information for you, Moomooboy said.

What kind of information? You have this time, Det. Browning asked.

The area where Liah's parents are staying, Moomooboy said.

How did you get the information? Det. Browning asked.

I overheard a conversation. A neighbour was talking to her next-door neighbour. They did not see me, i was hiding, Moomooboy said.

Ok, I am waiting, so tell me, where? Det. Browning asked.

They are staying in the village within half an hour drive from here, called Dalewoodville, at her brother-in-law, his name is Alfonso Singh. It supposed to be a secret, Moomooboy said.

Great, thanks for coming for the information. Are you walking back in the rain? Det. Browning asked.

Yes! I am, will change clothes, when i get home, Moomooboy said.

Here is fifty dollars for your information, but please stay safe, and away from the gang, Det. Browning said.

Thanks, I will try to find out anymore information, and come and see you. When I can, Moomooboy said.

Ok, bye for now, Det. Browning replied.

The information which Moomooboy gave was really needed, and in this way the detectives could make a trip to visit, and ask Liah's parents some questions about her where about the day before and what she did job wise.

I waited for the other two members of the team arrival, and let them know that I had received information where Liah's parents were staying, and asked them to pay them a visit, asking all the required questions pertaining to the case.

Although it was still raining, it was not coming down as it did earlier, so the two detectives left the station and were on their way to visit Liah's parents in the Village of Dalewoodville. The detectives located the house where Liah's parents were staying, knocking on the door. Liah's uncle opened it, and ask them to step inside. After introducing themselves, asked Liah's parents if they would answer some questions. Liah's mother replied yes!

Det. Haynes: Mrs. Singh, sorry for your loss. Can you tell me how old was your daughter?

Mrs. Singh: She was in her mid-thirties.

Det. Haynes: Was she seeing anyone at the time of her death.?

Mrs. Singh: Yes, she was. His name is Jack Kimble. They were in love with each other.

Det. Haynes: What type of work did your daughter do.?

Mrs. Singh: She was a schoolteacher.

Det. Haynes: What school was she teaching?

Mrs. Singh: She was teaching Brownstown Elementary School.

Det. Haynes: How long was Liah in a relationship with Jack?

Mrs. Singh: For about two years.

Det. Haynes: During that time, did they have any arguments?

Mrs. Singh: No, I have never seen them argue about anything.

Det. Haynes: Where does Jack Kimble live?

Mrs. Singh: He lives in Brownstown, at 96 Dalewood Drive.

Det. Haynes: Is there anything else you want to tell?

Mrs. Singh: Yes! My daughter helped an old lady nearby, in our village, before going to work and on week ends. She told me that the old lady wants to leave her the house, in her will, and not her son, who wanted nothing to do with his mother.

Det. Haynes: When did she tell you this?

Mrs. Singh: Two days before she disappeared.

Det. Haynes: We have identified the body that was in the vehicle, and traced it to your daughter, again we are sorry.

Mrs. Singh: Thanks. I feel an emptiness, since she went missing and did not come home.

Det. Haynes: Why do you say that

Mrs. Singh: She was always harassed by the gang where we live.

Det. Haynes: How long has this been going on?

Mrs. Singh: For quite a while, she did not feel safe anymore.

Det. Haynes: Why? Did she not report it to the police?

Mrs. Singh: She was threatened, that if she did, she was going to be killed.

Det. Haynes: Who threatened her?

Mrs. Singh: The old lady's son, who she helped.

Det. Haynes: Does he have a name?

Mrs. Singh: Yes, James Wilson, his nickname is "Skinny."

Det. Haynes: Thank you for cooperating with us, and hopefully, we can put the entire gang, and the drug lord, in jail.

Mrs. Singh: About her body. When would it be released?

Det. Haynes: We are going to call you as soon as it is ready.

Mrs. Singh: Thank you very much.

The two detectives, think they have as much information needed, and with the combine effort with the SWAT team, they can go into the Village of Junctionville, and arrest the four individuals, but it will be up for discussions when all three of them meet on their arrival at the station.

After the two detectives arrived at the station, and seated at their desk, detective Inspector Browning came into their office, and they both shared what they thought about the information they collected. The three detectives discussed the information Mrs. Singh provided, and after some lengthy talk, decided they will continue in the morning, leaving work, and returning tomorrow.

it's another day in the neighbourhood, and I got up earlier than normal, way ahead before the sun had risen, did some gardening, and clean the yard before my wife, and children got out of bed to get ready for the day which was in front of them.

I put away everything that was used in the garden and yard, walked into the house, and had a shower. After getting dressed for work, had breakfast, and was off to the station. The traffic was terrible because of a major collision on the Main road towards the station.

All vehicles had to make a detour onto another couple streets, which would bring me back to Main road, not too far from the police station, which was at 1144 Main road. The station parking lot was crowded today, with more vehicles than usual, and walking into the station, the duty officer at the front desk called me over. There is someone here to see you in the waiting room he said.

As i entered the waiting room, the gentleman stood up and introduced himself as Jack Kimble. Liah's boyfriend. I introduced myself, and told him to have a seat, and I will be back with him in a few minutes. I was not expecting any visitors, cause i did not make any appointment for today.

In the corner of my eyes, detectives Sargent's, Grant and Haynes walked in, and told them about the gentleman in the waiting room, and if they can take him back to the interviewing room, and hear what he has to say about Liah's murder.

The two detectives approached the visitors' room, introduced themselves, and asked Jack Kimble to follow them. After making themselves comfortable, it was time to hear what Jack Kimble had to say.

Det. Grant: When was the last time you saw Liah?

Jack Kimble: It was on Sunday at four pm, (4:00 pm)we had a date, went to the movies.

Det. Grant: What time did you drop her off after the movies?

Jack Kimble: Around ten thirty pm,(10:30 pm) stayed for a short time, then left for home.

Det. Grant: Did she ever mentioned anyone to you that may have threatened her?

Jack Kimble: No, but she told me someone was constantly harassing her.

Det. Grant: Did she say who, or what, it was about?

Jack Kimble: Yes, it was about land and house. The old lady she looked after was leaving her, but her son told her not over his dead body.

Det. Grant: Did she ever mentioned the name of the person who harassed her?

Jack Kimble: Yes! His name was James Wilson.

Det. Grant: Why? Did you not come forward when you did not hear from her?

Jack Kimble: I was threatened, that if i go to the police, I will not see the next day.

Det. Grant: Why now?

Jack Kimble: It's something I have been struggling with over the last couple of days, and that I should do the right thing, even if it cost me my life.

Det. Grant: Is there anything else we should know before you leave?

Jack Kimble: I don't think so. If I remember anything else I will call, and let you know.

Det. Grant: Did you two ever have sex?

Jack Kimble: No, we planned to, but not until we got married.

Det. Grant: Thanks for your honesty.

Jack Kimble: You are welcome.

The questioning and answering session with Jack Kimble was over. He was escorted to the front door entrance, and the two detectives went over the interview, trying to compare the information they got from Liah's mother, to see if it matched with each other, and to be honest, James Wilson's name was now a person of interest.

The detectives had lots of information on James Wilson that they could arrest and charge him with, but it was not the right time. It would be a joint approach, when things would be done by bringing all the four names they have on file arrested.

Meanwhile, Detective Inspector Browning was on his way to the school Liah taught, Brownstown Elementary School in Brownstown to ask a few questions, and answers by anyone who knew her, and how she got along with her colleagues.

At the school Detective Inspector Browning introduced himself, and was taken to the Principal Office and had a talk with Mrs. Jane Rivers the principal, they talked about Liah, as a very caring person, and the students at the school, loved her and so was her peers.

Detective Inspector Browning asked the principal to treat Liah's absence as being sick, and will let her know when she could let the whole school know what happened to her. The meeting with the principal at the school, and Liah's peers, was very positive, and was well received by Detective Inspector Browning and his team members.

The only thing standing in the way of making an arrest of the four gang members was the day and time the SWAT leader, and the detectives, would be given the green light to proceed. They did not think being assigned to this case felt positive until today, and thought this case would never come together. It was now had a positive spin solving it.

On my desk was a note with a phone number for me to call when i came in, and to my knowledge, the phone number is not one I could recall. After dialling the number, the voice seemed distorted, and the person at the end said, I have information about the case, and persons who abducted that woman and burn her in the farming Community of Carlson Point.

The individual wanted to remain anonymous, and he would leave a brown envelope at the corner of Avenue Street and William Street in the telephone booth. You should drive a police squad vehicle, so I would know that it's Detective Inspector Browning that is retrieving the envelope, and no one else.

Chief detective drove to where he was given the instructions about the envelope, retrieved it, and drove back to the station, opening the envelope. The names of two other men, along with the four men Moomooboy gave, were mentioned once again.

And the two added names involved with the abduction were Abdul Sardooh, the drug lord and Joey James, his driver, along with that information were pictures of all six men at a bar. The conversation and plans were heard to abduct Liah Singh and burn her body.

At present, the timing was not in their favour of proceeding with an arrest, even though the detectives now have the information in front of them. The phone rang, and the person on the other end asked to speak with detective Dan Browning.

This is detective Dan Browning,

This is Moomooboy, just calling to inform you of a conversation I heard. One of the gang member, James Skinny Wilson, will travel to Carlson Point tomorrow at ten am (10:00 am) to shop at Dollarwise. I am just letting you know he will be alone.

Thanks a lot Moomooboy, I appreciate everything you are doing to help with the case. Please be careful and stay safe.

After hanging up, detective Browning informed what he was told by Moomooboy, to his team, and was in discussions about staking out the store in the morning, after that meeting, all left for home calling it a day.

It's another day. I was smiling today more than the other days, knowing we were about to arrest one of the gang member, based on the information we received from Moomooboy; looks like it's going to be a great day one I will enjoy.

I was in a hurry to get dressed and get to the station, making sure that I will not be late, watching the Dollarwise store, hoping the gang member James "Skinny" Wilson would show up, so we could arrest him for the abduction and death of Liah Singh.

All three of us got to the station, walked into our offices, and discussed what procedure we were going to use. We all agreed one of us would be in the store pretending to shop, one would be at the back door, and the last one would be in the vehicle waiting for his arrival.

This procedure was accepted, and we all went separately to the store waiting for James "Skinny "Wilson's arrival. It was not long after arriving, and taking up our positions, the suspect, James "Skinny" Wilson, walked up to the store's entrance.

I gave the signal. The pigeon has entered the coop, and he was immediately arrested, and was swiftly handcuffed, placed into a police vehicle after his Miranda rights were read to him. He was taken into custody, placed into a holding cell at the station to be questioned, for not only taking part in Liah Singh's death and abduction, but all his outstanding warrants.

The detectives were in no hurry to question him, giving him sometime to think how we knew he was going to be at the store shopping. It was at least two hours after placing James "Skinny" Wilson in the holding cell. The detectives were ready to question him. He was led into the interviewing room, feet shackled and handcuffed, sat at the table waiting for the detectives to enter the room.

The detectives conducting the interrogation were Detective Inspector Dan Browning, and Detective Sargent Steve Grant, and Detective Sargent Victoria Haynes was going to watch on the monitor for anybody languages.

The both detectives entered the interviewing room, introduced themselves, and sat, making themselves comfortable, opening their files, looked directly at the accused, and Detective Inspector Dan Browning opened with these words.

Det. Dan: Is your name James "Skinny" Wilson?

Accused: Yes it is.

Det. Dan: Do you live in Junctionville?

Accused: That's correct.

Det. Dan: Do you know why you were arrested?

Accused: No sir,

Det. Dan: Let me jog your memory. Are you aware of the arrest warrants we have on you?

Accused: Ok, now I know, is that all those are petty things.

Det. Dan: No, that's not all. We also have information about your involvement in Liah Singh's abduction and murder.

Accused: Wow! Wait a minute. I was nowhere near or was involved in that crime.

Det. Dan: Are you sure about that? No questions.

Accused: I am sure, am not going down for something I did not do.

Det. Dan: If I told you, we have proof you were seen and heard talking about it. What would you say?

Accused: I would say you are all bluffing.

Det. Dan: They were six of you at a bar in Junctionville, and your conversation was overheard, pictures of all six of you were taken.

Accused: No way, you have any such evidence on me, or anyone else.

Det. Dan: Do you want me to show you proof? And you can hear the voices on the tape.

Accused: Ok, show me the pictures.

Det. Dan: I can also tell you the date. You all were at the bar.

Accused: You are really bluffing, your way of arresting me.

Det. Dan: Ok, let me show you the photos of all six of you. Abdul Sardooh, Joey James, Peter "Wide Mouth" Strong, Vernon "Skinny" Hinds, Winston "Big Belly" Walton, and yourself

Accused: Ok, yes, we were all at the bar drinking, and talking.

Det. Dan: Go on, we are listening to your explanation of the conversation.

Accused: She was a thorn in my plans. My mother, who was slowly dying, was going to leave the house and land for her.

Det. Dan: Why was that, and how did it come about?

Accused: She was always helping my mother before going to her teaching job, and because I was not helping, my mother told me she had changed her will. The lawyer had all the information.

Det. Dan: Did you planned, to abduct and burn her body?

Accused: I did talked about it, but did not kill her.

Det. Dan: Then who carried out the execution of her death?

Accused: I do not have any idea who did.

Det. Steve: You wanted her dead, and out of your way, didn't you?

Accused: I only talked about it, did not know it was going to happen.

Det. Steve: But it did, and that puts you smack in the middle as the killer.

Accused: I did not do it, I swear.

Det. Steve: Sorry, it won't work. You are guilty along with the others.

Accused: If i told you who did it, what's in it for me?

Det. Steve: I don't think there is anything in it for you.

Accused: Even if I told you who drove the vehicle, and abducted, and set it on fire?

Det. Steve: Not even what you say is true? I won't believe you.

Accused: Honestly, it's the truth.

Det. Steve: How many of you carried out her abduction, and burn her vehicle with her body in the trunk?

Accused: All six of us were involved. I only talked about killing her, because I did not want her to get the house and land my mother owned.

Det. Steve: You are just as guilty as the other five individuals.

Accused: I am sorry for all the trouble, putting her parents through with her daughter's loss.

Det. Steve: Are you pleading guilty of committing this crime, and by association?

Accused: Yes, if only I had kept my mouth shut.

Det. Steve: James "Skinny" Wilson, I am arresting you for the murder and abduction of Liah Singh.

Accused: Am sorry, so sorry.

Det. Steve: Get him out of here.

The accused, James "Skinny" Wilson, was led back to the holding cell at the station before he was transported to a minimum correction facility, while waiting for his case to be brought to trial in the court. It was a job well done, bringing at least the accuser to confess to Liah's death.

The arrest of James "Skinny" Wilson, seems like a good time for the detectives, and the SWAT team to go into the Village of Junctionville, and arrest the other five individuals, dismantling the gang, and returning the Village back to its normal state. It did not feel right.

I received a call from the pathologist, saying the body of Liah Singh was ready to be turned over to her parents. They would be happy knowing the detectives that visited her kept their promise. I made the call, and indeed they were delighted to hear the good news, and they can retrieve her body giving her a proper burial or cremation whatever they choose.

The day was a great success, as the case started seeing progress, but the element to surprise the gang was not there, the opportunity to go into the Village of Junctionville, and surprise the gang was lacking by the SWAT leader, objecting to the timing of the arrest of one of the accused.

We could not hold James "Skinny" Wilson for two days, and I related the information to the SWAT leader, he gave me, a definite answer it will be done in two night's time, if we can hold him over in the cell another night.

I told him it's a deal, but we have to move fast, before the gang realizes he was missing in the Village of Junctionville, and that may cause a problem for us. It was a positive sign, so I relayed the Information to my team members that they should prepare themselves for a raid on the gang. Thanking them for a job well done, we all left for home, to our families, all in good health.

It was a beautiful morning; the sun was bright, no clouds in the sky floating by, just a clear blue sky, and the occasional singing of a mockingbird in the Oak tree in the backyard. Today should be one with a positive outcome, with the SWAT team and my team carrying out a raid on the gang in the Village of Junctionville.

Trying to arrest the five other individuals in the abduction and murder of Liah Singh, although it was to be a day away, the decision was made to move it up a day earlier. At the station everyone was patiently waiting my arrival, and as soon as I got there, they were filled in with how the operation DRAWIT was going to proceed.

After the information of the proceedings, we all left for the Village of Junctionville to carry out the task, and making the arrest of the other five suspects. The raid of operation DRAWIT were twelve SWAT members, and the three detectives.

We got there before anyone knew what was happening, with tires screeching, and the SWAT members all converging on the homes of the know suspects. In a minute of a split second, three of the five suspects were arrested, but the drug lord and his driver escaped, but his vehicle was not in the garage.

Inside his house was searched, and a quantity of drugs found, which were confiscated, and the house was put under heavy surveillance. The house was thoroughly searched, and a secret room was found, which was a big surprise. It was a laboratory where he had drugs made with special chemicals, used to compel the user to crave more for the drugs.

Meanwhile, the three accused arrested were read the Miranda rights, taken to the station, and placed into individual cell away from each other, until the detectives returned to the station. While searching the drug lord's house, he left a bunch of important papers, which could be used as evidence against him. If caught, could send him to jail for a long time.

The evidence left behind by the drug lord was boxed and taken back to the station for safekeeping, also found was a picture of a house with no known address, which could be anywhere in the country. We all returned to the station after three hours, just a couple minutes before lunch, which was normally twelve o'clock.

We all had lunch and discussed who was going to interrogate which suspects. Each one of us will use unique skills to get the suspects talking before getting him to confess to the abduction and murder of Liah Singh.

Just before interrogating the suspects, Moomooboy called me with some good news. The people began coming out of their houses, and talking once again in the streets and their front yards. I told him thanks again for his help, and would definitely be in touch. He said goodbye and hang up the phone.

The first accused to be interrogated was Peter "Wide Mouth" Strong, which would be done by Detective Sargent Victoria Haynes, assisted by Detective Sargent Steve Grant. He was brought into the interviewing room, shackled and handcuffed.

The accused, Peter "Wide Mouth" Strong, stood six feet weighed around one hundred and fifty pounds with a scar on his right arm and a tattoo of a dagger on his left arm light brown in complexion and brown eyes. After sitting both Sargent's entered the room, introduced themselves, asked the accuser if he wanted water, he replied no, and Detective Sargent Haynes began her interrogation.

Det. Haynes: Is your name Peter "Wide Mouth" Strong?

Accused: Yes it is, you already know who I am.

Det. Haynes: It's for the interrogating records.

Accused: Ok, then get on with the questions.

Det. Haynes: Do you live in the Village of Junctionville since you were small?

Accused: Yes! I was born there.

Det. Haynes: Now that we have established that, let me come directly to the point. Did you or were you involved with the abduction and murder of Liah Singh?

Accused: No, was never there. She deserved what was coming to her.

Det. Haynes: Why did you say that?

Accused: She was always doing things for James "Skinny" Wilson's mother.

Det. Haynes: Is that a bad thing to help someone?

Accused: No, it's not, unless you are trying to get something out of it.

Det. Haynes: Like what, for instance, money, house and land.

Accused: House and land.

Det. Haynes: Whose house and land are we talking about?

Accused: James "Skinny" Wilson, that's what he told us a couple of weeks ago.

Det. Haynes: Are you sure?

Accused: Yes, I am positive. We talked about it at a bar the night before. She went missing.

Det. Haynes: Why do you say she went missing?

Accused: She has not been seen since. It's what I was told.

Det. Haynes: Do you know anything about it?

Accused: No, I had nothing to do with it.

Det. Haynes: What are you talking about?

Accused: Liah Singh, that's what I am talking about?

Det. Haynes: Have you seen James "Skinny" Wilson lately?

Accused: I saw him two days ago, not after that

Det. Haynes: Are both of you good friends?

Accused: Yes, we always do things together.

Det. Haynes: Did you and James talked about hurting Liah?

Accused: Yes, we did, while drinking at the bar.

Det. Haynes: Was it to hurt, or scare her?

Accused: To hurt her, James said.

Det. Haynes: And did he hurt her?

Accused: He did, one early morning.

Det. Haynes: What did James do?

Accused: He waited before she left for work, after visiting his mother's house, and hit her over her head.

Det. Haynes: What did he do after?

Accused: He placed her into her vehicle after gagging her mouth, called Abdul, told him he had Liah, and wanted to dispose of her body. All six of went, James drove her vehicle, and I

was with him. The others followed in Abdul's vehicle.

Det. Haynes: Where did he drive to?

Accused: We drove to Carlson Point farming community, parked her vehicle, and set it on fire.

Det. Haynes: You were a part of this crime, won't you?

Accused: Yes, I was at the wrong place and time.

Det. Haynes: Are you telling me you are guilty?

Accused: Yes, I am, just for being there.

Det. Haynes: Peter "Wide Mouth" Strong I am charging you by association of this crime, and you will return to your cell. You will be transported to a minimum correctional facility until your court date. Do you understand.?

Accused: Yes, I do.

The accused was led back to the cell and was waiting to be transported to the minimum correctional facility, where he will stay until his trial at court, a lawyer will be provided to him. The next accused, to be interrogated, was Vernon "Sneaky" Hines. He was also shackled and handcuffed as he walked towards the interviewing room.

He was tall, about six feet two inches, heavily built, with long brown hair, light in complexion, brown eyes, with a scar on the left side of his cheek. He was going to be interrogated by Detective Steve Grant and be assisted by Chief Detective Inspector Dan Browning.

After the accused was sitting comfortably, the detectives entered the room, introduced themselves, and the questioning began with these words from,

Det. Grant: Is your name Vernon "Sneaky" Hines?

Accused: Yes it is, have not changed.

Det. Grant: Have you always lived in the Village of Junctionville?

Accused: Yes, I have been, except in jail for a year.

Det. Grant: Are you familiar with the name Liah Singh?

Accused: Yes, what of it? That i should know.

Det. Grant: Who is she?

Accused: Some young woman I heard went missing from the Village of Junctionville.

Det. Grant: Do any of your friends know her?

Accused: Sure, most all of us guys know her, particularly James "Skinny" Wilson.

Det. Grant: How does James know her?

Accused: She helps his mother every morning before going to her work.

Det. Grant: Do you know the type of work she does?

Accused: Yes, she is a schoolteacher.

Det. Grant: How do you know she is a schoolteacher?

Accused: I heard it from James.

Det. Grant: Are you and James close, or not so close?

Accused: Not so close, but close enough as we want to be.

Det. Grant: Do you know anything about Liah's death?

Accused: Not really, I heard she is missing.

Det. Grant: Who told you she was missing?

Accused: From the whispering in the Village.

Det. Grant: Which Village is that, if you don't mind me asking?

Accused: The Village of Junctionville.

Det. Grant: Were you at a bar drinking a couple nights ago?

Accused: Yes, what is it to you, may I ask?

Det. Grant: Did James talked, about hurting Liah?

Accused: Not of my knowing.

Det. Grant: Are you sure, what if I told you, that someone saw you there while James spoke about hurting her?

Accused: I was not there when he mentioned it.

Det. Grant: Where were you?

Accused: I went to the washroom to relief myself.

Det. Grant: What if I told you I have proof you were there?

Accused: I would say you are bluffing.

Det. Grant: Are you sure I am bluffing?

Accused: I think so, you have nothing on me.

Det. Grant: Yes I do. (about to show him the photos)

Accused: Ok, I was there, and heard him spoke of hurting her, for trying to take what is his from his mother.

Det. Grant: Would you, as a friend, do anything for James?

Accused: What do you mean by anything?

Det. Grant: What I mean by that, is; would you kill somebody for James, if he ask you too?

Accused: Yes, and it depends, what it is about?

Det. Grant: Did he ask you to hurt Liah Singh?

Accused: Not in so many words, but yes.

Det. Grant: Were you with him, when Liah was abducted and killed?

Accused: Yes, she deserved what was coming to her.

Det. Grant: Why would you say she deserved what happened to her?

Accused: Because she wanted my friend's inheritance, and its way. Was it ever going to happen?

Det. Grant: Do you mean she had to die?

Accused: Yea, that's right, I am glad to be part of her death.

Det. Grant: Vernon "Sneaky" Hines, you are being charged for murder, and the abduction as an accomplice in the death of Liah Singh. Do you understand the charges?

Accused: In a sort of way, yes.

Det. Grant: You will be returned to your cell and be transported to a minimum correctional facility to wait on your trial at court.

The accused was returned to his cell, and is waiting to be transported to a minimum correctional facility, where he will remain until his trial in court, and will be visited by his lawyer. There is one last accused left to be interrogated, in the case, because it was getting close to the end of the day he was going to be interrogated the following day by Chief Detective Inspector Dan Browning. We all said good evening to each other and left the station.

This morning seems to come much earlier than normal. It did not feel I had enough sleep. Although I went to bed before my usual time. I may have been dreaming, but it was in fact reality, because the sun was in the sky, and the birds were chirping in the Oak tree in the backyard.

It's going to be a good day for me, because it's my turn to interrogate the last accused in the abduction and death of Liah Singh. I got dressed, had breakfast, and was well on my way to the station, when i got a phone call, and had to make a slight detour before reaching the station.

I arrived at the station half an hour after leaving home and was ready to interrogate the last suspect accused in the abduction and killing of Liah Singh. I asked for the accused to be brought into the interviewing room to wait on my arrival.

He was escorted towards the room like the others, shackled, and handcuffed, seated and waiting comfortably. I entered the room along with Detective Sargent Steve Grant, introduced ourselves, and Chief Inspector Dan Browning informed the accused he was going to conduct the interrogation.

The accused stood about five feet nine inches tall with a protruding stomach and weigh around one hundred and eighty pounds, dirty looking skin, brown eyes, a scar above his left eye and a tattoo of an anchor on his left arm.

Det. Browning: Is your name Winston "Big Belly" Walton?

Accused: Yes, it is.

Det. Browning: And You live in the Village of Junctionville, all your life?

Accused: Yes, it has been since childhood.

Det. Browning: Were you at a bar in the Village of Junctionville, the night before Liah Singh was killed?

Accused: No, I was not

Det. Browning: Where were you, if you were not there?

Accused: At a friend's house until late that night.

Det. Browning: Are you are sure it's your only chance to come clean?

Accused: I am sure about that night.

Det. Browning: Suppose I told you there is proof. You were at the bar the night before, what would you say?

Accused: You are lying and bluffing.

Det. Browning: Are you sure I am bluffing?

Accused: Yes, I am.

Det. Browning: What are you willing to wager?

Accused: If I win, you charge me, on a lesser offence, if I lose, then you can

charge me in the abduction and death of Liah Singh.

Det. Browning: Ok, (pulling out the brown envelope from the file, and about to show him some photos)

Accused: Wow! Hold on a minute here, how do I know it's not fake pictures?

Det. Browning: You don't. Are you still willing to go through with your wager?

Accused: Let me think for a minute. I think those photos are all fake.

Det. Browning: Let me show you what I have on all six of you? (showing the photos)

Accused: Man, I am in a hole, up to my neck.

Det. Browning: Why, do you say that, were you involved?

Accused: Yes, I was. How stupid of me to believe what James and the others said? We would not be caught for abducting and murdering Liah Singh.

Det. Browning: It was all lies, wasn't it?

Accused: Yes, it was.

Det. Browning: Tell me, what took place in the bar?

Accused: James came saying we should hurt Liah, for trying to take away what was belonging to him.

Det. Browning: What was belonging to him?

Accused: The house and land he grew up in.

Det. Browning: Why was that?

Accused: His mother told him she had changed her will, and was leaving it to Liah. He could not accept it.

Det. Browning: Go on, what happened next?

Accused: James planned to abduct her very early in the morning of her death by calling her about her mother needed help, which he did, with our help.

Det. Browning: How many of you were involved with her death?

Accused: All six of us, aided by borrowing a vehicle from Abdul Sardooh.

Det. Browning: Are you confessing to being involved with the abduction and murder of Liah Singh?

Accused: I am, and for that I am sorry about believing James, about not getting caught.

Det Browning: Winston "Big Belly" Walton, I am charging you in connection with the abduction and murder of Liah Singh. You will be transported to a minimum correctional facility, where you will have privileged to a lawyer, while you wait for your trial in court. Do you understand the charges?

Accused: Yes, sir, I do.

The interrogation took just about an hour and a half. He was led back to his cell the way he came into the interview room, placed in a cell away from the other three, accused, and is waiting to be transported to a minimum correctional facility.

The charges of abduction and murder of all four accused in Liah Singh's death are now awaiting their day in court, and it's up to the Prosecutor, and the Judge to set a date for their court trial. I hope in this case, the way the victim died, that bail for all four is denied.

And their trial date is not given, but they get a trial by a judge of the court who is a no-nonsense judge, who will give them the maximum jail time for crimes. It may be my thinking, but at least I can hope. The word, from what I have been hearing, is that the Village of Junctionville is returning to a bit of normalcy, and the people are going about talking once again as before.

I got a call from Moomooboy, saying Liah's parents are back at the house, and is keeping an ear out to hear where Abdul Sardooh, and his driver is located, but have heard no information about their whereabouts, and will keep in touch.

After getting off the phone, I felt good about the return of the people in the Village of Junctionville. The people were returning slowly to the normal state since the arrest of the four gang members for the murder of Liah Singh, and the evacuation of the drug lord and his driver.

In a couple hours, the day's work will soon come to a close, and a new day will begin eight to twelve hours after, then it will be a new day for work. It feels like the nights are not long enough for me. Maybe I am thinking ahead of the day to come.

It's another day, and all seems well, but is it, what is well for me may not be for others? The office was quiet when i got in, today is working on the paperwork on the accused. It's our duty to get all the paperwork along with the interrogation tapes, ready for the Prosecutor, so he can present it to the Attorney's office, and court dates could be arranged.

All three of the detectives, working together, making sure all evidence on the case, of Liah Singh's murder is done professionally, and handed to the Prosecutor's office in three days, so the Judge who is handling the case, can set a date for all four accused that is on trial.

Meanwhile, all four accused of the murder were taken one at a time and transported to a minimum correctional facility, and placed separately from each other so that they could not collaborate about their case.

In two days, we will attend the funeral and burial services for Liah, along with plainclothes officers, to watch out for any unwanted visitor, such as the drug lord Abdul Sardooh and his driver Joey James, all three of us who are working on the case.

Another aspect of our operation involves the continuous monitoring of the drug lord's residence, hoping that he will come back now that the people are returning to normalcy after Liah's death, and we can blend in with them.

The drug lord's house became the subject of discussion when the question of what to do with it arose, given the discovery of drugs. It was suggested the house should be seized, and turn it over as a satellite police station in the area.

It's not always easy putting the paperwork with all the evidence together. The process can be tedious, but they are standards and procedures which have to be followed, for the Prosecutor to understand, so he can make and find the accused guilty on all charges.

Although the work of getting all the evidence in this case is tedious, it had to be done. Sometimes it can put added stress on us, especially if we do not follow the procedures, and that could take a long time to complete. If we are given a certain number of days to get it done.

I think progress on the evidence with all four of the accused involved in Liah Singh's death should be ready for the prosecutor's office before the deadline, giving us time to think and concentrate on the funeral we have to attend as promised.

I have no inclination about Moomooboy, and what is his real name, or connection, but for now I will wait for him to tell us what it is, and recommend he get an award, for his bravery, and his constant observation, keeping us informed about activities in The Village of Junctionville.

Another day is winding down, slowly, and must say we are well ahead of presenting our evidence to the Prosecutor's office way ahead of our day and time. It's about time for us to leave work, everyone going their own way home after a long day's work, maybe to relax and chill in the backyard with our families.

The sunset was beautiful, as it dipped on the horizon, especially when half of the sun was showing, and before we knew it, the whole sun disappeared out of sight. The disappearance of the sun is now giving way to the night, as the streetlights came onto lighting up the neighbourhood heralding in what our night was going to be.

As the dark clouds roll in, the smell of rain felt eminent for sure. It was soon after entering the house, drops of rain started falling, and landing on the patio table that sat in the backyard. Then the rain came down as though someone opened the sky, and it felt like we were being bombarded with gunshots, but it was all the heavy raindrops hitting the table and the windowpanes.

As I looked through the front window facing the road, I saw the water from the rain flooding the drain, and then the loud peal of thunder, followed by lightning strikes with long streaks in the sky, and the strong wind gust along with the rain.

I closed the blinds before moving away from the window and sat for a while, before making my way to the bedroom, took a shower, and laid in bed. Thank God everyone was at home before all this started. The lights began flickering. Then they went off before that a loud noise was heard, a tree fell. Taking with it the electricity line at the corner of the streets.

It was a dark night, but luckily for us, we always had an emergency backup plan just in case lights went out, thanks to the person who invented candles. As the rain fell, we found ourselves in bed for the night, knowing in the morning they will be no electricity, to prepare breakfast, and we had to have our breakfast at the local diner.

In the morning, the sun came up bright as though nothing happened, but looking out, I could see a lot of debris of broken branches laying on the roadway like straw, shredded all over the road and also my back yard.

Just as I thought, there was no electricity and had to make sure all switches were turned off before leaving for work. It was slower than usual driving to work with all the cleanup taking place. It was reported no major damage was done, only the electricity was out in a certain section of the town.

The family had breakfast at the local diner, then off to our respectful destinations. The section where the police station was located did not occur any damage, and the electricity was still working. It was the topic of the morning. Everyone was talking about the night storm and the drive to work.

I listened to them verbalized for twenty minutes. Then it was back to work as usual, everyone doing what they were assigned to for the day. It was a good day, and it was time to complete the evidence for the Prosecutor's office.

The evidence for all four accused was done before we left for home, and I had the duty of driving to the courthouse, and handed to the

Prosecutor personally, before leaving for home, hoping he has everything needed, and nothing else was required.

The drive home was slowly returning to normal with the cleanup. As I head towards my home, the city was really on top of it, driving past. The electric company was doing their best to restore electricity to the neighbourhood where we lived.

It was going to take another couple of hours before the neighbourhood electricity would be restored. I ordered some Chinese takeout before my family arrived, making sure it would be hot when they came home.

The electricity was restored after supper. We sat and watched a movie, then went off to bed until morning. As the sun rose and showed its brilliance, splendour in the sky, it looked as though the day would be good for the funeral and burial services, which all three detectives had to attend.

Today is the day of the funeral. I got dressed and went directly to the funeral home, where the service was to taking place. I was the last to arrive out of the three detectives to get there. Some plainclothes officers were also there doing their duties, watching the building for any persons that were not welcomed.

The people began arriving, and one by one entered the funeral home, signed the book of condolence, before sitting down and waiting on the service to begin. The casket was sealed and was already there, as everyone walked in and flowers had adorned it on top and on the sides.

The service started on time, and after the rituals performed, the casket was taken to the place where remains of her body would be cremated, and her ashes placed in an urn and given to her parents. They were no reports of any unwanted individuals at the funeral home.

Just as we were about to leave, a young man walked up to us and said, hi, my name is Daryl Singh. I am also called Moomooboy Liah's nephew. Thank you for arresting my aunt's murderers.

Our jaws dropped in a moment of hearing who he was, and we could not quite picture the same person who came to us with information is the same person standing in front of us, thanking the three of us f for what we did for the family.

We walked away, knowing we did our best, and with the help given to us by Moomooboy at the time playing an intricate part in solving his aunt's death, bringing all the accused charged into the murder. I think it's only fitting he should get accommodation for all he had done. I will definitely put it forward to the Superintendent and discuss why he should get an award of this kind.

We returned to the station, and I immediately went to talk with the Superintendent about giving Daryl Singh accommodation for his bravery, and information solving this case of his aunt's death, and bringing charges to the four individuals that did the injustice to her.

The work day is turning out to be a short for the three detectives, since most of the morning was spent at the funeral service. We also had some things to take care of before leaving work for home. It's an hour left before we all left for our homes.

The phone rang twice before I answered. It was information I was waiting on, since the drug lord and his driver left the Village of Junctionville in a hurry. I had sent out an email to all the police stations within a six hours drive radius, about the picture of the house that was found at the drug lord's residence in the Village of Junctionville.

This was a positive sign for us. The conversation went back to the police station in the Town of Woodsworth, and the detectives there were given the authority to arrest Abdul Sardooh and his driver Joey James for dealing in drugs and for the sale.

I thank the detective from the Town of Comfortville, and hung up the phone. The information was passed on to the other detectives of my team, that the drug lord Abdul Sardooh, and his driver, Joey James, would be arrested the next day without him being aware of the situation.

He will need to be brought back to Carlson Point from the Town of Comfortville. The assignment was given to the Detectives Sargent's Steve Grant and Victoria Haynes to return the two individuals back. They would be accompanied by two heavily security officers.

The day's work was just about over, and the next phrase of another case was about to begin. The next day very early, the two detectives, along with the two heavily security officers, left for the Town of Comfortville, a six hours' drive, to bring back the two individuals.

It would not be possible to do the six-hour trip one way in a hurry and return the same day. The detectives and the security officers would overnight and leave early the next morning to return to Carlson Point.

It was okay with the department. I understood the arrest of the two wanted individuals went down peacefully without them know anything whatsoever a job well done by the detectives and the police of the Town of Comfortville.

I am looking forward to interrogate the drug lord (Abdul Sardooh), and hear what he knew about the death of Liah Singh, and also his driver's connection with this case, since it's not completed until all six men are convicted.

Their stories would be very interested to hear and their involvement in Liah Singh's death and what they did to stop it from happening to this young lady whose life was snuffed out when she was just start living her life in happiness.

The accused of the death of Liah Singh transfer took place, and they were on their way, where they would be held at the station cell, and interrogated the next day when it would be convenient to do so. It is not a priority, but it will give us time to prepare ourselves.

And the questions we need to ask them about some of their activities and gang members. I have to concentrate mostly on the drug lord (Abdul Sardooh) and questions I need to ask him, hoping he confesses, and I can get a conviction with what he says.

With charges from possession and distribution and Liah Singh's death. The two accused individuals arrived three hours after I got to the station. They were shackled and handcuffed, placed in separate cells from each other until it came for us to interrogate them the following day.

It's the morning, and the sun was shining as the birds chirp and hop on the ground, searching for worms. They were no sign of dark clouds or rain was forecast. All this could change on a dime, and what seems like a bright day can quickly change to rain,

I am looking forward to the privilege of interrogating Abdul Sardooh. The station was buzzing like bees when I entered. And talks about the two accused that were brought back after a couple days of disappearing from the Village of Junctionville.

They are sitting in our police station at Carlson Point, waiting patiently to be interrogated. I waited for my two team members to arrive and had a small meeting about how we think the interrogations should go. It was time to conduct our interrogating sessions. The first accused to be interrogated was Joey James.

He stood six feet two inches, weighed about two hundred and twenty pounds, scars on both cheeks, tattoos on the right hand of a gun and a dagger on the left hand, has long brown hair, brown eyes and grey eyes.

He was already sitting in the interview room when both detectives walked in, and the interrogation began after they introduced themselves. The interrogation was monitored by Chief Detective Inspector Dan Browning. The first to begin the interrogating would be Detective Sargent Steve Grant.

Det. Grant: Is your name Joey James?

Accused: Yes it is.

Det. Grant: And your home address is 135 Arnold Lane in the Village of Junctionville?

Accused: Yes, born and grew up there.

Det. Grant: Were you ever arrested? Yes or No.

Accused: No, I was never.

Det. Grant: Are you sure? I have evidence here saying something different.

Accused: Let me think, Yes! Coming to think about it.

Det. Grant: What were you arrested for, and how long ago?

Accused: It was three years ago, for drug possession and assault.

Det. Grant: Were you charged, and dis time in prison?

Accused: Yes, I was and released six months ago.

Det. Grant: How do you become Abdul Sardooh's driver?

Accused: One inmate who worked for him, before going to jail, told me about him.

Det. Grant: How long have you been driving for him?

Accused: For the last six months.

Det. Grant: Have you ever been caught?

Accused: No, not until two days ago.

Detective Sargent Victoria Haynes will now take over the interrogation of Joey James asking the questions, hoping she will get him to confess in the involvement of Liah's death.

Det. Haynes: What was your job description with Abdul Sardooh?

Accused: I was to deliver drugs to dealers, and pick up raw materials from his suppliers.

Det. Haynes: Were you both manufacturing drugs at his house for distribution?

Accused: Yes, we were.

Det. Haynes: Were you at a bar in the Village of Junctionville the night before Liah Singh's death?

Accused: I don't think so?

Det. Haynes: Are you sure I have evidence you five other individuals were?

Accused: I remembered that night.

Det. Haynes: What was the conversation about?

Accused: James "Skinny" Wilson was talking about hurting Liah Singh.

Det. Haynes: Do you have any idea what it was about?

Accused: It was something to do with his mother's house and land.

Det. Haynes: Go on, what about the house?

Accused: His mother was going to leave it in her will for Liah, and he could not have none of it.

Det. Haynes: Did you at any chance drive them after the abduction of Liah?

Accused: Let me think! Yes, I was. All six of us were at the scene.

Taking over the interrogating at this point was Detective Sargent Steve Grant, asking the following questions of the Accused.

Det. Grant: Who lit the vehicle on Fire, and who poured the gas?

Accused: Winston "Big Belly" Walton poured the gas, and James "Skinny" Wilson lit the matches that started the fire.

Det. Grant: You will be charged as being an accomplice to the murder?

Accused: Are you joking? I just went along as the driver.

Det. Grant: And you will also be charged, as an associate of the drug lord Abdul Sardooh?

Accused: This is not right, I want my lawyer?

Det. Grant: That can be arranged for you.

Accused: Oh, man, does that mean going back to prison again?

Det. Grant: Yes, it does, Joey James. You are being charged, of the murder of Liah Singh and associating with Abdul Sardooh in the distribution and manufacturing of drugs. Do you understand the charges?

Accused: Yes, I do.

The accused Joey James, was now charged and led out of the interviewing room, the same way he entered, shackles and handcuffs. He was taken back to his cell, waiting to be transported to another minimum correctional facility, away from the other four accusers during the day.

The interrogation of Joey James took about one hour and a half. It was discussed we take an early lunch before starting my interrogation of Abdul Sardooh. All three of us went to lunch at a restaurant close to the station that was in walking distance.

The three of us ordered and paid separately, Sargent Grant and Sargent Haynes ordered a burger and fries with iced tea, and I ordered fish and chips with iced tea. We had a seat and waited for our orders to be brought to us.

We ate lunch under an hour and returned to the station so I could begin my interrogation of Abdul Sardooh. I called the officer responsible for accompanying the accused that he should bring him into the interview room number two, and have him sit.

I will conduct the interrogation and Det. Sargent Grant will accompany me, and Det. Sargent Haynes will monitor the interrogation. We both walked into the room and introduced ourselves before we began our interrogation. Chief Detective Inspector lead the interrogating with these words.

Det. Dan: Is your name Abdul Sardooh?

Accused: Yes it is, since last I checked.

Det. Dan: Do you live at 41 Jackson Drive in the Village of Junctionville?

Accused: Yes, I do, for the last couple of years, after moving from Comfortville.

Det. Dan: Do you have any idea why you are arrested?

Accused: I think so, but not sure.

Det. Dan: Ok, let me inform you why you have been arrested? It's for the murder of Liah Singh, the manufacturing and possession of drugs.

Accused: Wow! Wait a minute. I had nothing to do with that woman's death, drugs yes.

Det. Dan: How positive are you about her death?

Accused: I am very positive about that.

Det. Dan: Think again. If I tell you, we have proof. You and five others were seen and heard plotting to hurt Liah Singh. What would you say?

Accused: I would say it was not me who was plotting to Liah.

Det. Dan: Your voice was heard saying to James "Skinny" Wilson to kill her.

Accused: That was not my voice.

Det. Dan: Yes, it was. It's time to confess about the killing.

Accused: I was nowhere at the scene of the crime, at the farming community of Carlson Point.

Det. Dan: I never mentioned where the crime took place?

Accused: I heard it mentioned, after the fact.

Det. Dan: After what fact?

Accused: After Liah's death.

Det. Dan: You were there, all six of you were present.

Accused: Who said?

Det. Dan: James "Skinny" Wilson.

Accused: Ok, Ok yes, I was present at the scene of the crime.

Det. Dan: About the manufacturing and distribution of drugs.

Accused: What about it?

Det. Dan: Would it be fair to say that you use your home to manufacture and distribute drugs?

Accused: Yes, that would be fair to say.

Det. Dan: Have you ever been charged with the possession of drugs?

Accused: Yes I was.

Det. Dan: How long ago, and did you do time in prison?

Accused: About four years ago, and did three years for possession and distributing.

Det. Dan: So you are familiar with being charged for possession and distributing of drugs?

Accused: Yes, I am familiar.

Det. Dan: What about being charged for the manufacturing and distribution of drugs?

Accused: Somewhat, I do.

Det. Dan: This is how it's going to play out. I need the names of your dealers and their addresses?

Accused: What's in it for me, after giving you their addresses?

Det. Dan: Absolutely nothing whatsoever?

Accuse: Then, I would not give you that information.

Det. Dan: Ok, Abdul Sardooh. You are charged in the murder of Liah Singh by association. You are also charged in the manufacturing of drugs and distribution. Do you understand?

Accused: Yes I do. Am going to beat all those charges.

Det. Dan: Good luck doing so.

The interrogation ended after one hour and forty-five minutes. He was taken back to his cell waiting transportation to a different minimum correctional facility until his court hearing. The murder of Liah Singh's accusers was all charged and waiting for the day of their trial.

As soon as it becomes available. The case is just about closed, but the last day this case ends is when all six men have been found guilty and sent to prison. This case began with little hope of ever bringing anyone to be charged and justice prevails.

It was a difficult situation, when no evidence or information was forthcoming, but thanks to a young man who thought he could not speak gave us the information he had gathered. I must give him credit for his bravery, and wiliness to do what it took to help with the arrest of his aunt's murder.

I hope after the trial and sentences are behind us, the Village of Junctionville will find healing, and the young man Daryl Singh would be given accommodation for his work in helping the police solve this case.

The day is finally to a close, and with the last two individuals accused of Liah's death, home is looking very gook, with a job well done by the three detectives. It was time for home. This is where I say good evening.

It's a beautiful morning. The sun was shining and streaks of light came through the window blind and casting it onto the floor. I had no trouble getting ready for work, and while eating breakfast, I began imagining. How my day was going to turn out.

The day was going to be filled with paperwork, which had to be completed, and handed over to the Attorney's office for the Prosecutor after the interrogation of the last two accusers in the death of Liah Singh.

In her death, we now have all the individuals accused and charged, and waiting on their trial date. It's our job to get the paperwork done and handed in as soon as possible, presumably by late evening before we all leave for home.

It's going to be to today that Abdul Sardooh and Joey James will be transported from the station cell to the minimum correctional facility waiting their turn to appear in court when the date is scheduled.

I am hoping, to be honest, their bail would be rejected, and they are tried by the judge without witnesses, to come forward on their behalf. I can only wish. Reality is not, it would not happen no matter what I wished.

The progress on the paperwork for the last two accused is close to be completed. The transfer of Abdul Sardooh and Joey James has now been taken place as we move forward, and hope to get their paperwork completed by the day's end.

It has been a week since the paperwork on the first four accused in the death of Liah Singh, and it is good to know a date for their trial by a judge has been granted, and bail was totally denied for all four individuals.

In two days, they will be in court standing in front of a judge who will ask them questions, and will make the final decision on their sentences. The judge I hope they face is the Honourable Judge Winston "no-nonsense" William, a judge everyone knows, is very hard-nosed with murder cases.

The three detectives in the case were asked to be prepared to appear in court the day of the trial for the first four accused, and also the two accused two days after. On that day for the accused James "Skinny" Wilson, Winston "Big Belly" Walton, Vernon "Sneaky" Hindes and Peter "Wide Mouth" Strong will know their fate.

And also if the judge is going to need answers from the detectives. It's another beautiful day, and the air smelt fresh as the birds chirped in the trees, and looking out the front window, school children were on their way to school.

Some children were laughing and shouting without a care about what was happening in the world. The day at work will start with the detectives going to court for the trial of the first four accused, and they will face the Honourable Judge Winston William.

At ten (10:00 am) sharp, the trial started with not any delays. The prisoners were led into the courtroom, shackles and handcuffed. They were accompanied by armed guards seated at the back of their respectful lawyers.

Patiently, the prosecutor sat down and awaited the opening of the judge's chamber door. The bailiff bellowed out all rise as the door opened and the judge sat in his chair, and said to be seated. The judge introduced himself as the presiding judge over this case.

Good morning to everyone he said, are we ready to begin this hearing? All four defence lawyers, and the prosecutor replied, yes, your honour. The prosecutor, in this case, was Mr. Trevor Babcock, and the lawyers were:

Mr. John Winger: Representing James "Skinny" Wilson

Mr. David Small: Representing Peter "Wide Mouth" Strong

Mr. Victor Bailey: Representing Winston "Big Belly" Walton

Mr. Alfred Harvey: Representing Vernon "Sneaky" Hinds

Judge: Let me come straight to the point. This is a straightforward hearing. There are only two answers I should hear, with no explanation whatsoever. It's yes or no. Is that understood?

All four lawyers replied with a yes, your honour.

Judge: Mr. Winger, the case of the abduction, and murder by fire. How does your client plead?

Mr. Winger: My client pleads guilty, your Honour, with full remorse.

Judge: Good for him. He should have thought about his actions.

Judge: Mr. Small, with the abduction, and murder by fire and by association. How does your client plead?

Mr. Small: My client pleads guilty, your Honour, and feels he was innocently coheres.

Judge: That's too bad. He should not have taken any part of it, since he knew what it was about.

Judge: Mr. Bailey, with the abduction and murder by fire, and by association. How does your client pleads?

Mr. Bailey: My client pleads guilty, your Honour, blamed himself for being in a gang with bad intentions.

Judge: It's good to know your client blamed himself.

Mr. Harvey, with the abduction and murder by fire and by association. How does your client pleads?

Mr. Harvey: My client pleads guilty, your honour, feels remorseful.

Judge: I am sorry to hear. How he feels?

As the presiding judge. I am going to say this; I have read the detective's interrogation, of all four accused, and I found it to be honest and justified the way it was conducted. I have also read the prosecutor's notes and outlines of the charges.

He thinks should be handed to each individual in the crime. I agree with him, but today as I hand down my verdict and your sentences. He wanted less prison time for each of you. In fact, I found what he had recommended was not enough, and I added five more years to your prison term.

I am not wasting the taxpayers' money, and have you return for your sentence hearing. The following terms would be for each of you for the abduction and murder of Liah Singh.

Judge: James "Skinny" Wilson, please stand. You are sentenced to ten years for the Abduction, twenty- five for murder by fire of Liah Singh's with no parole. You will spend your thirty-five years in a maximum correctional facility, giving you enough time to think about your actions.

The accused, James "Skinny" Wilson, was twenty-five years old when he was sentenced. He will be seventy years old. If he could remain alive, spending most of his adult life spent in prison.

Judge: Peter "Wide Mouth" Strong, please stand. You are sentenced to ten years for the abduction of Liah Singh, and twenty years for being associated with her death by fire. You will spend thirty years in prison, which should be long enough for you to think about what you have done with parole after twenty-five years.

The accused Peter "Wide Mouth" Strong was twenty-three years old when he was sentenced. He will spend thirty years in prison. Following a twenty-five-year sentence, he would be eligible for parole in the last five years. He would be forty-eight years, when his parole comes due, if he could live through his term in prison.

I don't they know what is in store for them, but where they are going, from what I understand, this correctional facility is one of the baddest in the country. I do not know how they are going to live through the ordeal there. Your guess is as good as mine.

Judge: Winston "Big Belly" Walton, please stand. The abduction of Liah Singh has resulted in a ten- year sentence for you, and your involvement in her death by fire has added another twenty years to your sentence. You will spend thirty years in prison, which would be enough time for you to think about your actions. You will be eligible for parole after serving twenty-five years, no sooner.

The accused Winston "Big Belly" Walton was twenty-eight years old when he was sentenced. He will spend twenty-five years in prison. Following a twenty-five sentence, he would be eligible for parole in the last five years of his thirty years' sentence. He would be fifty-three when his parole is due, if he can live through his prison term.

Judge: Vernon "Sneaky" Hinds, please stand. You are sentenced to ten years in the abduction of Liah Singh and another twenty years added to your sentence in the involvement of her death by fire.

You will spend thirty years in prison and will be eligible for parole after twenty-five years. This would give you enough time to reflect on your actions.

The accused Vernon "Sneaky" Hinds was twenty-five years when he was sentenced. He will spend twenty -five years in prison of his thirty years, and would be eligible for parole after twenty-five. He would be fifty-five when his parole is due, if he can make it through his prison term.

It was good to see justice prevailed for the deceased, and her family and was well served, knowing the four accused of Liah's abduction and death were convicted, and sentenced, which would send a message to those who are thinking about committing the same type of crime.

Judge: Would all four accusers please stand? You will be escorted to a maximum security correctional facility. You spend your sentence term there until your parole comes due, or your sentence term ends. Do you understand the terms of your sentence?

Yes, your Honour, the four accused answered.

The four accused prisoners were taken away, all shackled, handcuffed, and transported to the maximum security correctional facility called LAST CHANCE. A place where you make it or lose it, and where hardship starts the day, you enter the gates where you are housed.

It has been a day where the detectives can say they have done their jobs, charging the accused for the gruesome murder of Liah Singh and having them all convicted and serving prison time for their crimes. It is a busy day. We are all waiting for some good new on the other two accused.

It was another couple of hours after the sentencing of the four that we got the good new when Abdul Sardooh and Joey James would step in front of a judge to hear their case. I am hoping it is not by a jury but the same way the other four accused faced.

There is not much that can be done now, but wait for the day their case is scheduled. At the office, we spent our time going through any backlogged work we were working on before we three detectives were called to handle this crime.

As the evening sun began, its bow in the west, and the time for our day to end, I made a call to Liah's parents to share the outcome of the case, and her mother was satisfied with the sentences they were given. In her conversation, she mentioned the Village of Junctionville was coming around slowly the way it was before the drug lord and the gang had terrorized the Village for years.

I was glad to hear about the progress the Village of Junctionville was making. It was a sure sign that normalcy was slowly returning to a village that saw the hardship which was being controlled by a notorious gang.

The conversation ended when she said goodbye. Please keep in touch, about the other two accusers. I promised to keep her informed of their hearing and sentenced. It was just about the time to go home. After saying good evening to my colleagues, I left the station.

I knew it was a rewarding day's work. I took my time driving home, and was very surprised to see all my children and my wife at home. The table was set, and the food warming on the stove and in the oven. I greeting each one, sat on the couch for a while, and listen to them tell me about their day.

Before sitting down to have dinner told them about mine. After dinner, the dishes were cleared off the table. The sons washed and dried the dishes and my daughter put them away in their places. My wife and I sat on the couch relaxing.

When everything was done, and the kitchen cleaned, the children went to their separate rooms and did their homework. I took a shower and got ready for bed. It was a bit tiring day for me, and just wanted lay in bed with my wife until we both fell asleep.

As the morning sun began rising, the bright light shine through the trees, and the leaves twinkle, as the wind blew the leaves on the tree, making the light shine as though they were blinking Christmas tree lights. It was a magnificent view with such a spectacular view nature had displayed.

I took my time getting ready for work, sat and had breakfast before leaving. It was a slow drive and enjoyed the scenery as I drove along. After parking at the station took my time walking into the station, and towards my desk. I had to remind myself although things were slow, it can be change without notice.

I was just about to sit at my desk when the phone rang, and on the other end was the prosecutor letting me know that Abdul Sardooh and Joey James trial would be in three days, and we should get ready to attend the hearing, and be prepared to answer any question if called by the presiding Judge.

I ask him if it was a jury or trial by a judge, and he mentioned it was by a judge. All bail was denied to them. Good, I replied, and thank him before hanging up the phone. The other detectives came in just after I hang up the phone. I let them know about the trial date and the news of bail being denied.

It came as a surprise to me that news about the trial of the two broke so early, but my assumption is that they wanted to swiftly conclude the case without incurring expenses for the taxpayers. I am pleased about getting things over as soon as possible.

It would send a powerful message to all the drug lords, and gangs that are out there. You will be caught and will be tried without a jury and all cases coming up will be done quickly, placing no heavy burden on the taxpayers.

A little while later, I got another call from the planning department. The drug lord's house will be confiscated under the low of the state, and will be used as a police auxiliary station in the Village of Junctionville. All because of Liah Singh's death, and the arrest of the drug lord and his gang members.

There is not much work to be done today, but we had to stay focus, and get ourselves ready to appear at the courthouse in the next couple days. I kept busy by going through my notes and other evidence, and interrogation interview making sure everything was done the way it should.

The fact is going to court and testifying does not make me feel comfortable. If i do not have to go to the courthouse, it's all the merrier. It's the reason we all do our best at our job, to get everything prepared for any cases we solved.

Which has to be handed to the attorney's office the prosecutor needs. It's not every case you solve, you are going to be asked that your presence be there. If you are needed to testify in cases, preparation is the key to answering questions.

That could be presented to you by both the prosecutor and defence lawyers. The questions are different all the time. The way it can be put to you, and no matter how long you are an officer of the law, chances of you answering the question wrong can make or break your case, allowing the accused to go free, or with a lesser prison term.

It's something I learned from experience a long time ago, and was thought from an experience detective who I was working with. I never had the occasion to forget what he told me. Follow the procedures when you have solved a case, and you have to hand in the paperwork.

You will never lose a case when the paperwork is done right the first time. The day was coming close to the end of my working day. When it was time to leave the station for home. Looking through the window at the back of the station, the leaves began around by the wind.

The trees began swaying as the leaves began dancing as the wind blew stronger. As I looked further ahead in the sky, a dark cloud began forming, and knew it was going to rain sometime soon. The only thing left for me to do was leave for home before it all came down in a deluge.

Just as i entered my vehicle. The rain came down like cats and dogs and had to sit and wait until it became a little lighter before I could drive home. Just as it came down, so it left and a little sunshine showed up.

I had a great night's sleep, woke up in the morning feeling refreshed, and ready for work, but not before getting dressed, eating breakfast before leaving for work. The dread of going to court will be here, and am not really looking forward to seeing the faces of Abdul Sardooh and Joey James.

Who were involved, for Liah Singh's murder and abduction, and also the manufacturing of drugs and its distribution. I drove to work and all the while thought the judge presiding on the bench when they appear in court would be the Honourable Angus Marconi, a judge that would make them think twice for their actions.

There was nothing unusual about this day. Nothing much was happening at the station. Phone calls were few and no visitors, visited the station to make any complaints or report any accidents. The day went by just as fast as the morning came.

I was looking forward to going home, to relax and fire up the BBQ to cook some burgers and wings when my wife and children came home. It would be another fifteen minutes before i leave and reminded the other two detectives about court appearance in the morning.

I awoke this morning to the sound of rain hitting the windowpane and lightning flashing. The peal of loud thunder it was continued for at least an hour, before the rain stopped, but dark clouds still lingered overhead, and rain could start soon.

I got dressed, in a hurry, and grab two slices of toast and jam and out the door headed towards the courthouse for the trial of Abdul Sardooh and Joey James. The other two detectives on the team were parked and walking into the courthouse, were already seated, waiting for the trial to begin.

The two accused prisoners were escorted in handcuffs and shackles by two prison officers and sat behind their respectful lawyers.

Mr. Samuel Sampson lawyer for Abdul Sardooh

Mr. Keith Andrews lawyer for Joey James

Mr. Joseph Jackson prosecutor, who was handling the case.

With everyone in place, the judge's chamber door opened. The bailiff said, all rise, the Honourable Judge Angus Marconi presiding. The judge said please be seated. Just what I was thinking about who the judge would be came true.

Judge: Good morning to all. I see the accused are all present with their lawyers, and also the prosecutor. This is not a trial by a jury. It is going to be done by the confession that's in front of me. You are being accused, for the abduction, death of Liah Singh, drug manufacturing, and distribution. Are we clear?

Lawyers: Yes, your Honour.

Judge: I am not here to waste the taxpayers' money, and given all the evidence I have read, it is fitting to ask this question to both lawyers. Mr. Sampson, how does your client plead?

Mr. Sampson: He Pleads guilty your honour, but he has something to say. If you will permit him.

Judge: Ok, Mr. Sardooh, what do you have to say to this court?

Mr. Sardooh: Your honour. It was not my intentions to place myself with the involvement of this crime, but I did not think I was going to be caught for the other crime.

Judge: Thank you. It was your choice to put yourself at the scene of of the crime, with your other members. Please remain standing, Mr. Sardooh, after reviewing the evidence and confession of these cases. I am sentencing you for ten years in the abduction and an added ten years for murder by association. In the manufacturing of drugs, there are fifteen years involved, and an additional ten years in the distribution of drugs.

Judge: You will spend forty-five years in prison, and will be eligible for parole after spending forty years. Do you understand?

Mr. Sardooh: Yes, your honour.

Judge: Be seated.

The age of Abdul Sardooh was thirty-five and will be seventy-five years old when his parole comes due if he can survive while in prison.

Judge: Mr. Andrews, how does your client plead?

Mr. Andrews: He pleads guilty your honour.

Judge: Mr. James, please stand. In reviewing the evidence, and confession, I am sentencing you for ten years in the abduction and an additional ten years for murder by association in the death of Liah Singh. In addition, another ten years for the helping in the manufacturing of drugs and another ten years for distribution of the drugs. You will spend forty years in prison, which time you will be eligible for parole after thirty-five years. Do you understand?

Mr. James: Yes, your honour.

Judge: Be seated.

The age of Joey James was thirty years of age and will be seventy years old when his parole is due, if he can survive while in prison. The two prisoners were escorted out of the courthouse the same way they entered after the judge left the bench.

We were satisfied with the terms of their sentences, and when it is published by the news medias, I hope it would deter some drug lords and gang members to think twice about their involvement dealing with illicit drugs.

As detectives, try to solve any crime could be tough. They cannot be easily solved without the information from its citizens. We are very grateful for a courageous young man who kept us informed, making it possible for us, bringing all six individuals to justice.

Before they could carryout more of the same crime the way it was done to Liah Singh. Finally, it was a day to celebrate. We went to our friendly restaurant, ordered pizza and wings, then talked about the case and team work. It was a pleasure working alongside Detective Sargent Steve Grant and Detective Sargent Victoria Haynes.

If it was not for Moomooboy, we could have never got this far in the case. It was his constant watching, and listening to what the gang members were saying and doing, and giving us the pictures and movement. It was made possible for us to apprehend the accusers in Liah Singh's abduction and murder.

We are glad this day has finally ended, with the results of the case, so we could all go home to relax and wait for another crime that needs solving. Today was a wonderful day for all. The justice system sends a stern message that it could be still trusted to uphold the law.

After we returned from our lunch and before leaving for home, I got a call from the attorney's office saying Daryl Singh would get accommodation for his bravery helping us solve the crime. I also made a call after hanging up with the attorney's office to Liah's parents.

I informed them about the sentencing of their prison terms, and she was satisfied that the justice system worked, but still misses her daughter. She had faith all along that the six individuals would be punished to the full extent of the courts.

The next morning, after arriving at the station, I got a surprised visit from Daryl Singh. He had three envelopes in his hand. He was inviting the three detectives to a community event in the Village of Junctionville, on April,28/2001 at 11:00am, and wants us to be there.

They want to show us their appreciation for getting things back to a normal state now that the six individuals responsible for his aunt's murder are in prison. I accepted the invitation on behalf of the other two detectives, and he left thanking me for a job well done.

It's now my turn to make sure that his accommodation can be done on the same day the Village was having the community event. This would be a great day and time to do the presentation, letting the Village know what a brave individual they have living among them.

I was given the green light that his plaque would be ready in time for the event. It was Saturday, the community event in the village of Junctionville was taking place today. During this day, the detectives and their families were eager to be present and wouldn't miss it for anything.

The event was well planned, and we all met Liah's family before the presentation of the plaque to Daryl Singh. As the crowd began gathering around the stage as the music began playing, and the announcer asked Daryl Singh on to the stage.

It was a complete surprised to him when the Superintendent of Police came forward after he was standing, wondering why he was called on to the stage. The superintendent, Mr. Jack Foster, asked for silence, and said, Mr. Daryl Singh on behalf of the police department, it is an honour to present to you this plaque of accommodation for your bravery in helping solve the crime of your aunt's death.

We all stayed for the event, enjoying the day and talking to lots of people in the community. The children all enjoyed themselves and made friends with Daryl before leaving. The day ended on a friendly note, and the sound of music said it all.

The event went on hours after leaving with not any incident, because of the police presence mingling in the crowd. Three months after the community event, the auxiliary police station underwent a complete renovation and reopened.

The station was staffed by six officers and included the use of two police vehicles. They were a constant surveillance of any unsavoury persons that were not living in the area.

The official opening day of the police station in the Village of Junctionville was going to be on the Saturday where the people will be invited to the opening and tour the building.

The police were making sure that no drugs or distribution of it ever happen again in the area and was keeping a sharp eye in the area. They were now trained using drones to help with patrolling the area which they can do where no one is aware of them.

In the couple of months in the village, the people came to know the officers personally and had good rapport with them. The children were now looking forward to the police visits to school, talking and reminding them what drugs can do to their system.

A few months after the police station's open house, Daryl and five of his friends approached the Sargent in charge at the station, Sargent David Greene. How can we help? In what way do you mean? I mean, how can we help watch our village? We thought about forming a group to watch things when you cannot.

Do you mean like a village watch? Yes? Daryl replied,

Let me talk to the superintendent and hear what he thinks about the idea.

Ok Daryl said.

The boys left the station, positively hoping the Superintendent would approve the idea. Two weeks after the proposal, the Sargent called Daryl and his friends telling them that the superintendent approved their idea, and they will have to be trained in a few weeks' time.

The boys were so happy and excited to help keep a watch on their village. They could not wait to start their training. Which will be done at the police college for two weeks. They would be trained by one of the best, and after training, could use the station to meet with the Sargent in charged.

They were also trained on how to operate a drone and navigate it in different conditions when the is bad. It was an excited time for the boys and after their two weeks' training graduated. Their task would begin in a couple weeks and the people in the Village of Junctionville were very proud of them.

The Superintendent was also proud of them and asked the head of the police college to allow him to present their certificate at the police station in the Village of Junctionville. There the people can come to see them accept their certificate.

The Village of Junctionville police went around announcing a special accusation that would take place on Monday at the steps of the station and requested their presence. Finally, the day arrived for the boys to receive their certificates. The Superintendent Jack Foster, Detective Chief Inspector Dan Browning, Detective Sargent Steve Grand and Detective Sargent Victoria Haynes were present.

They were all proud of the boys, and along with their certificates, were each given two sets of clothes that identified them as the Village Watchers Association. Their uniforms were yellow t-shirts, black cargo pants and black baseball caps with a crest on the front VWA.

After the small ceremony, they were given a shout out for the encouragement, wanting to make the Village a better place to live. The boys were enthusiast about starting their duty, and the Sargent brief them on where he wanted them to concentrate in a special area of the Village.

Although the boys were still in school soon to graduate, they considered the police force as an alternative if they could not find work after graduating. It was a decision they sat and talked about and since they were familiar with the police school, it would be easy for them to pursue a career in the police force.

They still had a couple months left before graduating, and continued their village watch when they can in the evening after school and Saturday and Sundays. The boys would have to decide soon about their future because the application for the police college would be in a couple of months.

The boys gave it lots of thought. Two of the boys were thinking of joining the fire department, and Daryl and his other two friends, the police department. The day for filling out the application forms, they went to each department and fill out the forms and had to wait for a week before they got a reply.

A week after filling out their applications, they were all accepted to the department they applied to, and they going to basic training in two weeks' time. The boys were cheerful that they were accepted, and all because of their two weeks' training at the police college when they formed the Village Watchers Association.

The news spread through the Village of Junctionville like a raging wildfire, that the people were glad that the boys choose to become police officers and firefighters. The first of the youths in Junctionville. It was now up to the Village of Junctionville community to continue with the Village Watchers Association before the boys left for their training.

It was not surprising, the amount of young men that came forward who pledged to continue with watching the Village of Junctionville where Daryl and his friends left off. The boys were given a great send off to training, and the three detectives were there to wish them well, on becoming police officers and firefighters.

The Village of Junctionville was now in skilled hands because they were now most of the village keeping watch daily. All this activity stemmed from Liah Singh's death, which made it possible by the courageous act of her nephew.

It is said; it takes a village to rais a child, but it looks like the other way around where it took a young man to raise a village. This was not the intention of some fluke. It was all made possible when the drug lord and the gang members who were controlling the Village of Junctionville were arrested and sent to prison.

The village is now in a more stabled state, and everyone is walking around safe and in a relaxed frame of mind, knowing that they are not controlled by anyone but themselves. It's been two weeks since the boys left the village and the words on the street were that they are all doing great.

It's been three months since the drug lord and the gang members were in prison, and a couple of young ladies in the village were now taking care of James "Skinny" Wilson's mother, but she was not doing too good. The doctors gave her about three weeks to live.

Mary Wilson, James "Skinny" Wilson's mother, changed her will and stated that her house should be called after Liah Singh. It should be turned into a small community centre where the children of the village can come together and learn how to engage with each other.

I am not surprised that she would do a thing like that, since Liah was the one who took care of her for years before she was abducted and finally murdered. Mary got worst after changing her will and the village people of Junctionville took turns sitting at her bedside, daily and praying with her.

It was not enough to say Mary Wilson died in her sleep at the time her doctor predicted. The Village of Junctionville has lost a generous woman and a great elder in the community. The ladies of the village had everything prepared for her funeral, because she had left the details of how she wanted to be buried.

Unfortunately, James "Skinny" Wilson was informed of his mother's death. He would not be given anytime to attend her service and burial. The day of the funeral, five boys from the Village of Junctionville returned and were the pallbearers of her casket.

They were dressed in their uniforms and the people were glad to see them paying respect to the deceased. It turned out that the police department in Junctionville was present also, and the three detectives showed up to pay their respects. The funeral service was packed at the church and they were standing room outside, as people listen.

After the funeral service, people gathered at the house and were served drinks and food to eat before going back to their respectful homes. It was the talk of the village that her own son could not make the service because of the choices he made in his life.

The boys had some time off for the funeral before they had to leave the next day, but everyone was glad to see them. The detectives were also glad to see them and talk about their training at the police college. In a matter of months, they would have gone through everything they need to know at the police and at the firefighters' colleges.

The entire village of Junctionville was proud of the boys and had good things to tell them about the Village Watch Association they started, and how much it has grown to where everyone in the village was part of it.

After several months of intensive training at both the police and firefighters colleges, the boys will graduate and would be placed in a station where they would serve the public as official police officers and firefighters.

It was Daryl's tenacity that gave him the courage and bravery in the solving of his aunt's death and it's this push in him to become a police officer because of her, and the friendship he had with Chief Detective Inspector Dan Browning. The relationship he had with the inspector led him to pursue the career of an officer of the law.

Training at college is finally over, and in three weeks, the boys will graduate after a long eight months of hard work studying, and will soon be called police officers. The days, weeks, and months are now moving at a fast pace. And the time for the boys graduating will be here.

The entire village of Junctionville is now waiting for the day of their graduation when they come home to show their appreciation by throwing a big event on the weekend they arrive home. Invitations to the police officers in the village and the three detectives were also invited.

Finally, graduation day is here and the parents of the boys at the police and firefighters college were present to see them accept their diplomas, and send off home as police officers. The police officers were dressed for their graduation in white pans with a red stripe down the sides, black shoes, white shirt with black ties and a white jacket, and a black police hat.

The boys at the firefighters' college were dressed in black pants, black shoes, red shirts, black ties and red jackets with firefighters helmets. Both parents of the two boys were proud of their children for the career choices they made.

The graduation ceremonies were well attended. Detectives Browning, Grant and Haynes were also there to witness the coming of age for the person called Moomooboy, whose real name is Daryl Singh.

It was a proud moment to see him on stage after marching to the sound of the band.

He graduated with top honours in his class and his two friends were runners up. The village boy who became a police officer today who was not sure he was ever going to become a police officer, and is now the first to be one of three in the village.

Now that the boys are home after the ceremony, they can relax for a bit, but the people of Junctionville are about to give them a party, showing their appreciation for becoming a career person with a future ahead of them.

The day of the party, all five boys were taken out after lunch for a couple hours so the people can decorate the grounds where the party are going to take place. They were not aware of what was in store for them. It was all going to be a surprise.

And what a party it was when they arrived back at Junctionville. The banners were put up all around, showing their appreciation just for becoming police officers and firefighters. A village that is proud of its community that is now safe so that they can walk around freely without being fearful.

The boys are now treated with respect, and so did every person in Junctionville, something that was lacking throughout during the drug lord and his gang controlling the village, people were afraid to talk with each other for fear that they were conspiring against the drug lord and the gang.

As the party continued, they were several speakers wishing the boys good luck in their careers. Inspector Dan Browning made a speech which started this whole turn of events by talking to Daryl, when he was known to the gang as Moomooboy. The chain of events has now turned around where Junctionville has taken back control.

The celebration of the boys went on well into the night and no one from outside the village of Junctionville except families were allowed. They were no incidents reported during or after the celebrations, which was great for everyone to know.

The village was once again in excellent hands, knowing the satellite police station was a deterrent to anyone who wanted to come and try starting any illicit drug activities. Now that Junctionville was back as the community, it once was is now considered a blessing.

The three boys that graduated from police college wanted to talk to Inspector Dan Browning. They got dressed and went to Carlson Point Police station to see him about becoming a detective. Entering the station and as they walked to the duty officer's desk, they were already identified as future officers.

They all said good morning and asked to speak to Inspector Dan Browning.

Don't I know you he asked?

Yes, sir, you do, replied Daryl.

Wait, let me page him for you, the officer said.

Thanks, I will, said Daryl.

The boys had a seat in the waiting room for inspector Dan Browning to see them. He was elated to see the difference the first day Daryl walked into the station looking all dinge and wet with information about his aunt.

Inspector Dan Browning introduced himself to the other two boys before asking them some questions.

Inspector: What brings you boys here?

Daryl: We just wanted to drop by and ask you a couple of questions ourselves.

Inspector: What do you want to know?

Daryl: How did you become a detective?

Inspector: After joining the Police department, I saw the way they dressed, with a suit.

Daryl: What made you want to dress in a suit?

Inspector: I thought it command respect, beside that, I went to college and took courses that would enhance my career as a police officer.

Daryl: Ok, how long did it take you to graduate after enrolling in college?

Inspector: About three years. Why did you ask?

Daryl: I am thinking of becoming a detective one day.

Inspector: Good for you. I will help you anyway I can when you are ready.

Daryl: Thanks,

Inspector: Where would you boys want to be stationed ?

Daryl: I would like to be stationed at Carlson Point police station.

Mike: I would like to be stationed at Junctionville.

Harold: I would like to be stationed at Junctionville.

Inspector: I wish you boys all the best on your appointments. Don't forget to let me know where you are going?

Daryl: We will let you know as soon as we know something?

Inspector: Bye, and thanks for the visit.

The boys left Carlson Point police department happy after talking to Detective Inspector Dan Browning. It was the answer they wanted to hear about becoming a detective and what the need to achieve in becoming one.

Before going home, the boys went to the mall and had lunch at the food court, watching young ladies walk by and comparing them to each other. It was a fun day for them because after all the fun is over, they will have to get serious about their work.

Returning home to the village of Junctionville, the boys went to the police station and visit with Sargent David Greene, and the rest of the police officers there. It was a friendly gesture, knowing one day they may work with him.

It was something two of the boys are hoping for to be stationed in a community they are familiar with and the people all know them when they were growing up as children. They are all acquainted with the people in the area and it will be a bonus if they can actually work in the community.

Two days after visiting with Chief Detective Inspector Dan Browning, the boys received their job information about where they would be stationed. They were all surprised when they opened their letters and found out their wishes came true. Each got exactly the place they had hoped.

They all had to report to their station on the Monday of the following week. After knowing where they will be stationed, Daryl called Detective Inspector Dan Browning to give him the good news, and he would see him on Monday morning when he report to the dispatch officer.

After calming down, the boys went out and celebrate at the local restaurant, eating and having some mild drinks, not to get themselves drunk. They celebrated for a couple of hours, then left the restaurant for their homes to relax and sleep off the drinks.

The other two boys that went to the firefighters' college were also assigned at their home base of Junctionville and had to report there on Monday, so all the five boys were all stationed where they can do much good for the community in Junctionville.

It was the start of a beautiful day for everyone of the boys knowing that they got their wish, and they would serve a community where they lived, making sure the village of Junctionville will always be safe in the future without being run by any gangs.

All five boys got together that evening, met under the tree and talked, where they see themselves in three years' time, but none of them talked about getting married. They were all focused on doing their jobs. They were called to where are placed.

Talks went well into the late night as they celebrated what they have accomplished in the eight months. It was getting late, and the boys said their goodbyes to each other, promising to see each other every day until the day came for reporting to their place of work.

It was Saturday, the beginning of the weekend, and all five of the boys got together with some other friends at the river for a swim and picnic for the whole day, some girls were present old friends from their school and everything went well for all that were there.

The boys knew this was going to be their last time together, so they were making the time spent together worth their friendship, and making the best of the day and their time. Everyone had a good time and as the evening approached, they knew it was time to say their goodbyes.

Its Sunday morning and some boys slept in after their long day by the river, and were not in any hurry to venture outside but remain and rest as much as possible because the following day they had to report to their workstations, to begin what was their career choice.

Life will be different now that the boys are now working daily. It's a bright morning, and they were no clouds in the sky. According to the meteorologist, no rain was predicted all day for the inaugural first day for the new recruits as they report for work.

I am sure they are going to be nervous, but it's expected since it's their first day on the job. They will be trained not by textbooks but on the job where life is faced daily and what they may have learned in text-books are thrown out the window, observing what real life is daily.

As officers, they will have to learn how to use their instinct, be observant, and judgment when they are in tough situations. Each one of them will be trained by an original officer for the next couple of months until they feel confident to be on their own and can handle the situation they are involved with.

The first day of of training was not too bad. The boys had different scenarios played out in front of them, on their shift, which they handled it as though they were veterans, but in the days to come, they could be a little difficult, not so much for Mike and Harold but for Daryl.

Because Daryl is stationed at Carlson Point, there is more violence, robberies and assaults. He has to be aware of all the situations involved that can put him in danger if not careful. The boys have to get used to the three different shifts they have to work.

Training for the night shift would differ from the evening and day. Each one will teach them what to expect and be aware of, but most of all, they have to prepare them self for the scenarios that are going to be played out in real-life situations.

Two weeks of training has been completed and boys had a day off to compare what they had learned, and exchanging information about it. They were confident that they are going to be great officers and move up in ranks as they are going to be going to college to further their education in the police department.

Another morning for the boys as new police recruits begin another week of training, and they are so looking forward to it. The one most looking forward to it was Daryl. He was in the town of Carlson Point police station and his training was more intense that the other two that were stationed in Jacksonville.

Today, his training will have to do with traffic control and tracking speeders using the radar system. After this week of training, he will be out with another officer and applying what he has learned from the other officers who trained him.

What he has learned will come in handy when he has to be alone and make a judgment call that requires his knowledge as a police officer. He had a surprise visit from Chief Detective Inspector Dan Browning, wanting to know how it was going for him and, if it was all that he hoped, it would be.

His answer to Inspector Dan Browning was yes, and he was glad to be a police officer. In his conversation with the inspector. He wanted to know more about furthering his education on becoming a detective, and what courses he needs.

Inspector Dan Browning advise him to wait for another three months when he feels settled in doing his job and will talk again, and give him the advice he needs to pursue the courses that would advance his chances of becoming a detective.

Daryl tanked the Inspector and went back to work with his training officer for the rest of the day. After writing out his daily report, left the station and drove home, stopping in at the station in Junctionville to see Sargent David Greene. He wanted to just talk and ask a couple of questions.

Sargent Greene gave him some encouragement to not give up on his dream, that he should pursue it with a passion no matter how hard it looks. Now six months have gone since he last talked to Inspector Dan Browning. He is in an excellent position to ask about the courses he needs to take at college so that he can become a detective.

It was his dream, ever since he met Chief Detective Inspector Dan Browning, and wanted to be like him in a certain way. He got all the information he needed, and he began planning the month he was going to start his college education to make his dream a reality.

In the fall that year, Daryl started his college education pursuing his dream of becoming a detective. He worked hard at it even after working at his job, whether during the day, evening or night he did what he had to do, although he knew it was going to be tough.

Knowing that he wanted to be a detective, after fourteen months of hard work, he finally took his last exam of the course and passed it with the highest marks in the class.

He was happy that all his hard work had paid off and was positioned someday to apply for a position in the Carlson Point police department as a detective. Upon his graduation, he was congratulated by his friends, Chief Detective Inspector Dan Browning, Detective Sargent Steve Grant, and Detective Sargent Victoria Haynes.

Little did he know that something was in the works for him, but this was going to be a surprise not only for him but for Chief Detective Inspector Dan Browning, Detective Steve Grant, and Detective Sargent Victoria Haynes. They were not aware that Superintendent Jack Foster was retiring at the end of August.

The person to replace him was going to be Chief Detective Inspector Dan Browning, and they would need another detective within the Department, and this was his chance to get the position as a detective. His chances were favourable. Now it was a wait and see what would happen.

The months flew by, and it was announced Superintendent Mr. Jack Foster would be retiring, and that the new Superintendent would be Chief Inspector Dan Browning, Detective Sargent Victoria Haynes position would be Chief Detective Inspector Victoria Haynes, Detective Sargent Steve Grant position would now be Detective Inspector Steve Grant, and joining the team will be Detective Constable Daryl Singh.

After the announcements, everyone was congratulated, and welcome the newest member of the detective team, Detective Constable Daryl Singh. This was his day to show the world that with persistence, anyone can make it with hard work and the dedication they put into themselves.

He has proved to himself that if he wants something so bad, hard work has to be done. With all the congratulations over, it was time for the workday to begin, and his first agenda was to read how the department prepare their reports.

His mentor, while on the job, will be Superintendent Dan Browning, who was Chief Detective Inspector at the time Liah Singh was brutally murdered, and the person who was known as Moomooboy is now transformed to become Detective Constable Daryl Singh.

During the day, Chief Detective Inspector Victoria Haynes called a meeting to update everyone of her detectives about the day's duty. Nothing has changed except that of the new position, which was filled by Detective Constable Daryl Singh.

Another day's work has come to a closed, but before going home D.C Daryl Singh went to speak with his mentor Superintendent Dan Browning, to thank him for believing in him, and that he would do everything to uphold the standards of being a good detective.

After their conversation, he left for home follower closely by the Superintendent. As he walked out into the open air said to himself, Yes, Yes, Yes I did it and smiled knowing that was where he belongs, doing what he know was the right in his eyes and his aunts.

The Village of Junctionville saw the spark in his eyes when he got home, and hearing his good, all that knew him came and congratulated him on his hard work over the last couple of years. They all knew that his aunt would be proud of him for the way he had turned out.

As the people left his home, he had time to take all this hoopla about him now being a detective, the first in the Village of Junctionville, and it may not be the last. Because of this, he may have shown other boys what anyone can become when they put their mind to accomplish whatever they want out of life.

As the evening sunset into the west, the lights in Junctionville came on and the quietness brought the sense of peace that it was not felt for a long time. The night was as quiet as can be. No traffic was heard and everyone was in their homes enjoying the calmness of the Village.

At the break of day, those who were jogging or just walking waved as they met each other. The Village of Junctionville now has a reputation as being the safest in a three-mile radius, all thanks to the dismantling of the drug lord and the gang that once lived there.

Today is the first official day on the job of Detective Constable Daryl Singh. He does not know it, but there is a scene being played out on his way to work where he has to take charge of the robbery that would take place when he walks into the grocery store.

His police training would have to kick in gear. As he entered the grocery store noticed the confrontation and immediately his instinct about what to do next came into play without hesitation, tiptoed up to the robber and with his quick reflexes disarmed the offender, arresting him.

His quick thinking saved the cashier's life. This was his first arrest as a detective, one that he could put on his record as being in the right place at the right time. It turned out the robber was wanted for another robbery at another grocery three days ago, not too far from where he was arrested.

The robber was taken to the cell at the station and was interrogated by Detective Inspector Steve Grant and assisted by Detective Constable Daryl Singh. They were both satisfied with the statement of the accused and he was taken to the courthouse where the day court was proceeding. He was given six months in prison for his crime.

It was the first time D.C Singh ever went to court and saw what it was like to be sitting and hearing lawyers plead for their clients. I am sure they will be more cases that he will have to be present for in the years to come, during the life span of his career.

He was congratulated on his return at the station, but was talked to by Chief Detective Inspector Victoria Haynes. The next time he should have waited for backup, but she understood his position that he had to act fast before it escalated.

Just after talking with Chief Detective Inspector Victoria Haynes, I walked back to my desk and before I was about to sit, there was a called it was heard over the police radio of shots fired at the corner of Green St and Evans Lane, and one person was lying on the ground, with multiple gun shots to his body.

The assailant fled the scene in a vehicle driven by another person. The detectives were on the scene, along with the ambulance and other police officers. Shortly after the police arrived, the scene was taped off and the detectives on the scene asked if they were any witnesses.

The victim was taken to the hospital but died on arrival. He succumbed to the bullet's wounds. The scene is once again being played out the same way that Liah Singh died in a way where no one wanted to come forward to give us any information.

The detectives approached the different businesses to see if they heard anything or have any security cameras installed, but they simply refused to answer any question for fear of being called a rat. It can be a stigma that can stay with you for life.

From what we know, the hospital does not actually know who the deceased is at the moment, not until the coroner and the pathologist came up with his identity. This investigation could take a while, since no one wants to hand us any information.

The fact is, there was a murder, and yet with all the witnesses that saw what happened, everyone present in the area where the shooting took place refused to even talked to the police. It's typical. People simply do not want to help the police in any way when a murder occurs.

The questioning and looking for clues were concluded. Now the detectives have to wait and see if anyone would ever come to them with information about the shooting. The investigation will continue and meanwhile, the detectives will look through their database to see if they are any criminals out of prison in the last couple of months.

It will be some time before we hear from the coroner and the pathologist, but we will wait for confirmation until we know exactly who the person is. This will give us a chance to look for his name in our database and see who he was associated with or if he was a dealer selling drugs and owed anyone.

As for D.C Singh, he is learning the ropes pretty fast. His life was forced into a reality situation and is in the process of learning that a case is not solved in a day, but it could take months. He is now seeing how why his aunt's case took that long to solve.

At this time, he is in a good place to learn from the best and become a good detective where he can change in other people's lives. I hope he understands the ramifications of being a detective. He has to be open to what is thrown in front of him and deal with it as it comes into his life.

He may not like it sometimes, but it's what being a detective goes through, seeing dead bodies in all shapes and forms and in some gruesome manner. This kind of job is not for the faint of heart. It's a life of horrors and will have to live with it until he retires.

The case is still not solved, and the investigation continues. Who knows when it will be solved only by the detectives in the case, when they can get the information they need? Could this be a cold case for another department to solve?

We may never know how this case would turn out. Maybe it would be solved by Detective Constable Daryl Singh when he becomes a Detective Sargent in the future.

About the Author

Father of two children, with three grandchildren, and a greatgrandson comes from a family consisting of three boys and four sisters.He interest are fishing, hiking,and walking. He resides in the City of Mississauga, Ontario Canada.